# A LITTLE SPARK

# ALSO BY BARRY JONSBERG

*Catch Me If I Fall*
*A Song Only I Can Hear*
*Game Theory*
*Pandora Jones (Book 1) Admission*
*Pandora Jones (Book 2) Deception*
*Pandora Jones (Book 3) Reckoning*
*My Life as an Alphabet*
*Being Here*
*Cassie*
*Ironbark*
*Dreamrider*
*It's Not All About YOU, Calma!*
*The Whole Business with Kiffo and the Pitbull*

# BARRY JONSBERG
# A LITTLE SPARK

ALLEN&UNWIN
SYDNEY·MELBOURNE·AUCKLAND·LONDON

First published by Allen & Unwin in 2022

Copyright © Barry Jonsberg 2022

All rights reserved. No part of this book may be reproduced or transmitted in any form or by any means, electronic or mechanical, including photocopying, recording or by any information storage and retrieval system, without prior permission in writing from the publisher. The Australian *Copyright Act 1968* (the Act) allows a maximum of one chapter or ten per cent of this book, whichever is the greater, to be photocopied by any educational institution for its educational purposes provided that the educational institution (or body that administers it) has given a remuneration notice to the Copyright Agency (Australia) under the Act.

Allen & Unwin
83 Alexander Street
Crows Nest NSW 2065
Australia
Phone: (61 2) 8425 0100
Email: info@allenandunwin.com
Web: www.allenandunwin.com

A catalogue record for this book is available from the National Library of Australia

ISBN 978 1 76052 692 4

For teaching resources, explore www.allenandunwin.com/resources/for-teachers

Lyrics from 'Annie's Song': words and Music by John Denver
© Copyright 1974 BMG Ruby Songs/Reservoir Media Music/Mushroom Music
All Rights for BMG Ruby Songs administered by BMG Rights Management (US) LLC
All Rights for Reservoir Media Music administered by Reservoir Media Management Inc
Print rights for BMG Rights Management administered in Australia and New Zealand by Hal Leonard Australia Pty Ltd ABN 13 085 333 713
www.halleonard.com.au
Used By Permission. International Copyright Secured. All Rights Reserved. Unauthorised Reproduction is Illegal.

Cover & text design by Debra Billson
Cover images by Shutterstock: Iaroslava Daragan/Sewon Park/Studio Ayutaka/mBelniak/Artist Vaska/Anna Sol/tereez
Set in 12/16pt Sabon by Midland Typesetters, Australia
Printed in May 2022 in Australia by Griffin Press, part of Ovato

10 9 8 7 6 5 4 3 2 1

The paper in this book is FSC® certified. FSC® promotes environmentally responsible, socially beneficial and economically viable management of the world's forests.

www.barryjonsberg.com

*For Cathy Hood and Jude Lee*

My name is Caitlyn Carson, but you can call me Cate or CC.

This is mainly about me. I'm thirteen years old and not especially remarkable, which, I know, is not the most compelling reason to read on. But it's not *only* about me. I have parents that play significant roles in this story. My father is Michael Carson and he loves me. My mother is Lois Houseman and she loves me. They don't love each other. I suppose they must have at some stage, but if so, no one talks about it. Now they just nod or exchange neutral words, and I think if it wasn't for my presence (and I am *always* there when they are together) they would make judgements about the other's character and possibly resurrect old wounds or grievances. Worlds of pain lurk there. Keeping all that in check is tiring. Sometimes I feel resentful that I was given the role when no one asked me if I wanted it. Most times I just feel tired.

I love my parents, so that's good.

But sometimes I think love isn't enough. Even though I'm only thirteen years old, which, let's be honest, does not add up to an impressive lifespan, I've learned that love isn't necessarily what it says on the pack. I know it can inject pain, destroy lives, twist people into shapes that quickly turn monstrous. In some ways we'd be better off without it.

I suppose that's what this story is about. Love, pain and the mysteries that are people.

It's also about madness and why we need it.

# CHAPTER ONE
★

It was dark, it was late and I had no idea why Dad had driven us out from the city for over an hour. I'd seen dark and I'd experienced late.

But Dad normally has his reasons.

Normally.

When I tried to discover them, however, he wasn't completely forthcoming.

'It's just a drive, okay, Cate? Into the Dandenongs to a secret place I know.' He glanced over at me and gave a chuckle. 'Actually, it was a place I used to go to with your mum. When we were courting. And a good few times after we'd stopped courting and got married.'

'No one uses the word "courting" anymore, Dad,' I said. 'Not if you're under a hundred anyway.' I didn't want to discuss the rest of his statement. *Courting*, as I understood it, meant trying to impress the other person with how wonderful you were. Did that stop once you got married? Apparently, from Dad's point of view, it did. I found that sad.

'In fact,' said Dad, 'we came up here slightly over thirteen years ago.' He reached over and punched me lightly on the arm. 'This place I'm taking you to . . . well, it's possibly where you came into being, Cate. Know what I mean? Isn't that worth the trip?'

It only took half a second before the meaning hit me.

'Oh, yeew,' I squealed. 'That is so gross, Dad.'

'But . . .'

I stuck my fingers in my ears and started humming. I glanced over from time to time and he was smiling, but he wasn't talking so I unplugged my ears.

'What's so special about this place that it's worth driving for . . .' I glanced at my phone. '. . . sixty-seven minutes?' I stabbed at him with a finger. 'And nothing about what you and Mum got up to, okay?'

'You'll see,' said Dad. 'You'll see. Unless I got this seriously wrong, we should be getting there in the next couple of minutes.' He muttered to himself, 'About twenty minutes past Kalorama Park, on the left . . .'

If I'm going to be honest, I was starting to get grumpy. We'd left at nine in the evening, and it was now nearly ten past ten, so even if we got to the place, turned around and headed home, it would be close to midnight by the time I hit bed. I know how sad that sounds, but I was tired, okay? And grumpy.

I opened the passenger window and stuck my head out. It was so dark out there. It was strangely unnerving to be travelling down a narrow, winding road with just the headlights to show the way. They cut a tunnel in the darkness but didn't show much of what was to each side. The night air was cool and smelled like trees and earth. I tilted my head and looked at the sky. The branches of trees whipped by, but in those moments when the sky was clear I could see the dusting of millions of stars. Wherever we were stopping, the night sky would be fantastic. You don't really get to see the Milky Way properly when you're close to Melbourne. Humanity has washed it away with streetlights and football stadiums and television sets.

But out here?

Out here there was no filter. The universe stared down at us and it was naked and brilliant and never-ending.

Dad finally stopped the car at the side of the road and we got out. It was really quiet apart from the ticking of the engine as it cooled. Dad opened the boot and handed me a blanket, took out a torch and a wicker picnic basket and locked the car.

'Just down this path here, Cate.'

I could barely see the path, even with the torch, but I grunted and followed him through a small gap between two bushes. We stumbled down a rutted track for probably no more than ten metres and then Dad turned off the torch. I gasped.

We stood on a clearing at the top of a rocky outcrop. The Milky Way coiled above us, a vast ribbon of points of light, some red and orange and white and yellow and all the colours in between. Far off, glittering in the light of a quarter moon, was a band of water.

Dad put his arm around my shoulder. I shivered a little because it was cold.

'Worth the drive, Cate?' he asked.

I just nodded.

'I don't think many people know this is here,' said Dad. 'I found it by accident.'

'Don't tell anyone,' I said. They'd only put up viewing platforms and pay-for-view binoculars and vans selling convenience food.

'Our secret,' said Dad.

We stood for a few minutes and I *did* know that this was worth the drive. It was worth getting back at midnight. Why was I being so bitchy? It was Friday night. I wasn't going to be up at six thirty in the morning. I wasn't going to be up in the *morning*.

'It's amazing,' I said. No words could capture what was above my head. No words I could find, anyway. When I managed to tear my gaze from the lightshow above, he'd laid out the blanket on the ground and opened up the picnic basket. There were two insulated containers with a couple of coffee mugs.

I love my dad.

I sat on the rug, hands warmed around my coffee mug (mine was hot chocolate – did I mention I love my dad?), leaning back and staring into the infinite. I couldn't remember the last time I'd felt so calm, so . . . at one with everything.

'We're time travelling, Cate,' said Dad. 'See that star up there?' I tried to follow his finger, but everywhere you looked there were stars. In fact, there was no place in the sky that wasn't saturated with them. 'It's red. See?' I thought I could make out a red star in the vague direction he was pointing. And I guessed it didn't matter if I saw it or not. He could and he was going to tell me something about it.

'Yes.'

'That's Betelgeuse. It's in the constellation Orion and it's six hundred and fifty light years from us, give or take. A light year is a measure of distance . . .'

I knew what a light year was, but it would've been rude to interrupt.

'. . . the distance light would travel in a year is about nine and a half *trillion* kilometres, so that star is roughly six thousand trillion kilometres away from us. This means we see Betelgeuse as it was six hundred and fifty years ago. The light coming from that star, the light hitting our eyes now, started its journey around the year thirteen seventy odd, when Shakespeare wasn't even a glint in his father's eye.'

He stopped, possibly to allow me to absorb what he was saying. I knew something about this stuff, but it was still exciting to hear it and experience it at the same time.

'The Milky Way,' he continued, 'the galaxy we call home, is about one hundred thousand light years across and contains around one hundred billion stars. The universe – what we can see, at least – contains probably two trillion – two million million – galaxies a bit like the Milky Way.'

The numbers were starting to become meaningless. They do when you talk about the night sky, but again, I just liked hearing dad talk. The air was clear and cold, the stars were the same and I felt the entire universe was looking down at me, my hands wrapped around a metal cup of cooling hot chocolate. It was the strangest feeling.

'We live,' said Dad, 'on an unremarkable planet next to a totally unremarkable sun at the unfashionable edge of an unremarkable galaxy in a universe teeming with galaxies.' He paused. 'How does that make you feel, Cate?'

'Not gonna work, Dad,' I replied. 'I'm still the most important thing ever created.'

He laughed.

'Know what?' he said. 'I think you might be.'

Which is when I saw the light. It was one light at first, and for a while I thought it might be a shooting star. It was off to my right, at the border of my vision, and it must have been the movement that caught my attention. It travelled quickly for a second or so and then stopped dead. I might not be an astronomer, but celestial bodies don't behave that way. Do they?

'Did you see that, Dad?'

'Hmmm?'

'Over there.' I pointed. 'That bright white light.'

Dad gave a small chuckle. 'A white light, huh, Cate? Well, that narrows it down.'

'It's that...' But the light had changed colour. It morphed from white to orange to red and then to blue and back to white. And it moved leisurely in a straight line from right to left. I didn't say anything else. I could tell by the way Dad gripped my hand that he'd seen it too.

'It's a UFO,' I said.

'You are so out of touch, Cate,' Dad replied. 'They're called UAPs now. Unidentified Aerial Phenomena. But I think you'll find a simple explanation for it. It's probably the International Space Station.'

'Changing colour?'

'Maybe. Maybe it's picking up light reflecting from the upper atmosphere. There are all kinds of crystals up there, Cate, with all kinds of chemical composition. It's how astronomers discover what stars are made of, by analysing their light spectrum. I'm sure that's all it is.'

I pointed my finger.

'The International Space Station seems to have stopped dead now, Dad. Oh, they've found reverse apparently...'

I wasn't trying to be sarcastic. The words just came out. The light had changed again, cycling through a different set of colours, and as I'd pointed out to Dad it was performing some really weird manoeuvres, reversing rapidly, staying still for a moment, darting up and down.

'Maybe it's a drone,' said Dad.

'There's another one. Over there.' Another light, far to the left had appeared, moving slowly but steadily towards the initial light. Then I saw another one. And another. Six in total, seven, nine, twelve. They converged on each other, morphed into a pattern against the sky. A diamond formation, each dot of light sparkling in a different colour. It was amazing and exciting and slightly, just slightly, scary. I didn't know if the tingle down my spine was fear or sheer joy.

'That would be a lot of drones, Dad,' I said. 'And what would be the point? To impress a couple of people in a deserted place?'

'Your theory then, Cate?'

'Those lights are coordinated and moving in a way that cannot happen in nature. They are controlled, they are designed. There's intelligence behind them.'

'And?'

'And that intelligence is either from here or it's from there.' I waved a hand at the sky in general.

'I thought we'd get to aliens sooner or later,' said Dad. 'That's a very long bow you're drawing there, Cate.'

'Is it?' The lights suddenly broke apart from one another, spread out in a line across the sky. The one in the very centre grew in size. Or at least that's what my eyes were telling me. Then I understood. It wasn't growing, it was approaching. The tingle down my spine increased. Part of me wanted to run, another part needed to know what was going to happen next. To be honest, it wasn't much of an internal battle.

The light now resolved itself from a blur into a disc. There was no doubt that this thing was a disc and that it was spinning – the shifting formation of colours a consequence of a different face being exposed to my line of sight. I still had no idea of its size because there was no reference point to help me. Against the backdrop of the universe, this thing could have been a metre in diameter or a hundred metres.

I realised I'd stopped breathing. I forced myself to take long, steady breaths. I could feel my heart thudding against my chest.

In less than ten seconds they all disappeared. They just winked out of existence. We spent ten minutes searching the sky, but all the lights had gone.

'Looks like the show's over,' said Dad.

'Not necessarily.' I'd read enough about flying saucers or UFOs or UAPs to know that they could be back at any moment. It was late in the evening and I had no pressing engagements. We could afford another half an hour to see if they'd come back for a curtain call. So we sat on the rug. There was no more hot chocolate in my thermos but Dad let me have the rest of his coffee. It was pretty disgusting, but it was hot.

'Aliens?' said Dad. 'You were going to explain.'

'You pretty much said it yourself,' I replied. 'Countless billions of galaxies with countless billions of stars, yet we think Earth is the only place to have intelligent life? That's crazy, Dad. It's crazy from a mathematical point of view as well. Probability alone says there must be millions, possibly billions of intelligent life forms out there, most more advanced than our own.'

'So where are they?'

I waved a hand at the sky. 'Hello, Dad. Haven't you been paying attention?'

'Ah, I see. These aliens have travelled countless light years in their crafts, in defiance of the laws of physics, to arrive here. And then what? *Hey guys, we've just travelled for two million years. Let's scare the crap out of those two humans and get the hell out of here. We can laugh about it all the way home. God knows, we'll have time.*'

'I don't know what goes through an alien mind, Dad,' I said, though his remarks stung a little, maybe because they made sense. 'I don't know what goes through yours most of the time.'

'Me neither,' he said. 'C'mon. Let's get going. I'm starting to get really tired and you've just drunk the last of my coffee.'

We packed up and walked to the car. I was going to lie down in the back seat, but Dad insisted I recline the passenger seat as far as it would go. At least that way I could use the seatbelt. He put the heater on full and we started to move. I'd even closed my eyes when the car lurched to a halt and the engine went quiet.

I opened my eyes to the car's bonnet and interior bathed in a weird orange light.

Something was above us. I could see the rays of light around the bonnet, and outside, to my left, parts of the surrounding bushes were illuminated as if by a torch. We were pinned by a beam of light from whatever was hovering above. I listened but there was no noise.

'What do we do, Dad?' I whispered. I glanced over at him. He sat forward in his seat, trying to look up into the sky, eyes squinting against the light.

'Stay calm, Cate,' he said.

'Should we get out of the car?'

'I don't think that would be a good idea.'

I was relieved. I didn't think it was a good idea either. But the notion of sitting here and not doing anything also wasn't very appealing.

Suddenly the light blinked out. One moment we were in a spotlight, the next in total darkness. Dad turned the key in the ignition and the engine started. He put the headlights on full beam and turned onto the road. I arched myself as far to my left as I could, but the angles weren't right to see much through the passenger window and I really didn't want to wind it down and stick my head out. Neither of us said anything until we'd driven maybe a couple of kilometres.

'Could you see anything above us?' I asked.

'Not a thing.'

'What the hell was that?'

'I'm touched, Cate, that you still think I might have answers. For this, I haven't. I've no idea what we just experienced.'

'It'll be beyond cool when I'm back in my bedroom. Right now, I'm scared.'

We drove in silence for another couple of kilometres and then Dad laughed.

'The joke?' I asked. My eyes were starting to droop.

This had been one of the most exciting nights of my life, but my body had decided it had had enough. I was beginning to shut down.

'Just checked my watch,' said Dad. 'You'll be pleased to know we haven't lost any time. You know. You hear about people who lose hours and then, through hypnosis, discover that aliens abducted them and performed experiments.'

'Anal probes, mainly,' I replied.

'They wouldn't want to probe my anus,' said Dad. He started laughing again and it took a second or so before the smell hit me.

'Dad, that is so gross,' I said, winding the window down and putting my head out into the cold night air. Being abducted by aliens was better than keeping my nose inside that car.

# CHAPTER TWO

★

'And you didn't take pictures on your phone? Videos? You know, like any freaking normal person would've done?' The last five words built in volume, so that the final syllable was a blast in my ear.

I hate Elise sometimes. Most times I love her.

'I know. I'm an idiot.'

'True that, CC.'

'But I didn't think. At the time I was too busy watching, you know?'

'You didn't think? True that, CC.'

We have a very strict routine at lunchtimes, me and Elise, and it goes beyond where we sit and what we eat. We have five minutes of having a go at anyone we feel like, from singers to actors to teachers to fellow students to each other, leading in to a frank discussion of what is going wrong and right with our lives. In this, we have to be brutally honest. I don't think we ever talked about that as a rule or a routine, but it's kinda accepted. We tell each other everything. Well, nearly. I knew today that Elise had something important on her mind. It was my job to drag it out into the open. Anyway, I was anxious to get beyond my UFO experience, which only proved, apparently, that my self-proclaimed stupidity was drastically understated.

'What's the problem, Elise?' I said.

'My life's turning to shit,' she said.

'Specifics? Everyone's life is turning to shit. What makes yours special?'

'I got this feeling Mum and Dad are getting a divorce.'

Ah. Now here was something I knew a lot about. For once I'd actually be able to give advice without feeling like a fraud.

'What makes you think that?'

'''Cos last night they said, "We're getting a divorce."'

I couldn't help it; I nearly pissed myself laughing. To be fair, Elise howled with laughter too. It's one of the things that makes us so close – we have a very similar sense of humour.

'Your lines of deduction oft seem like magic, Sherlock Holmes,' I said when I'd calmed down a little. We giggled a bit more.

'I'll tell you what they said then, if you like,' I continued. 'They said that they both still loved you more than anything in this world, that their split was nothing to do with you and that they will do everything in their power to ensure that you remain the absolute focus of their lives.

They may also have said that they couldn't regret their relationship because it produced you, but that the time had come to find happiness apart. They don't hate each other, in fact they hoped to remain good friends and they won't do anything to punish the other. It's blame-free and all for the best. How am I doing?'

'Freaking amazing, to be fair. Is it *all* bullshit?'

'Absolutely not,' I said. I picked at my salad, tried to find more chickpeas. 'They mean every single word. *Now*. The trouble is in the future when they start to think the other is getting away with stuff or has got a better deal or – wait for it – another partner. Watch out for that, Elise. That's a helluva time.'

'That's what happened with your mum, yeah?'

Mum and Dad split up seven years ago and the conversation I predicted with Elise's parents was pretty much what had occurred with mine. The thing is, they believed it. I believed it. It was the truth. Until Sam came along and swept Mum off her feet. My parents must have predicted that something like this would happen – was *bound* to happen, sooner or later. Might've been Mum, might've been Dad. Just happened to be Mum. Sam was a personal trainer at the gym that Mum joined a couple of months after the divorce came through. I know! It sounds like a plot line in one of those shocking soaps where everyone is obsessed with image and, it seems, everyone else's partner. Maybe she should have recognised it for a cliché and taken up another activity. Lawn bowls, maybe. Full-contact crossword puzzles. She didn't. She took up

Sam and he took up her. Within a couple of months he'd moved in and the bathroom smelled of sweat and cheap cologne.

I like Sam. In fact, he's great. Right from the start he made it clear that he wasn't going to try to be a father to me. I knew this because he and Mum sat me down and hammered that point home.

'I'm never going to try to be your father, Cate,' he said. 'You have a father. I know that and I respect that. You are their child, not mine, and I know I have no power over you, nor do I want any. I just hope to be your friend; that you'll look at me as someone who, in time, you might trust, maybe even confide in.' He held up a hand. 'Though I certainly don't expect that. Do you think we could try to be friends, Cate?'

What could I say? Of course I'd try. But I had no power in this and we all knew it. He'd come to live in my house and there was no veto available to me. He was a walking, talking symbol of my lack of control.

They'd obviously told Dad, because when he picked me up for our fortnightly weekend at his place he was overly cheerful, smiling all the time and talking in a voice that was way too perky. Nothing was going to crack through that facade of sheer joy at what cards the world had dealt him. But later, when I couldn't sleep, I heard his sobs through the thin partition between our bedrooms. The sound cut me like a knife.

I shook my head. Elise, way back when, had asked me a question. I tried to remember what it was.

'Oh, yeah. Sam. He suddenly became a player in a game beyond all our understandings.'

'He screwed things up?'

'No.' I thought about it. It's not often you're forced to think about things like that. 'No. He's a nice guy. Even Dad thinks so. But he was a force of change and that, by definition, I guess, threw us all out of our orbits.'

'I reckon Dad's got another woman,' said Elise.

'Then brown stuff might be about to hit a fan,' I said. 'Keep your head down, is my best advice.'

'Did you have a good time with your dad this weekend?' I hadn't seen Sam when I got back late on Sunday. Mum normally asked Dad to get me back by eight in the evening, so I could shower, get everything ready for school and get a decent night's sleep. Dad always swore he would, but normally it would be after ten by the time he dropped me off. He was always very sorry about it, though.

Sam was busying himself in the kitchen making dinner, which smelled pretty amazing, I have to say. Mum was going to be home late because there was a parent/teacher night at the school where she teaches. Sam does most of the cooking, even when Mum is here. I was finishing a small bit of maths homework at the dining table, and put down my pencil.

'Yeah. Great, thanks,' I said.

'Did you do anything fun?'

Now, here's the thing. I could have told Sam about the UFOs or whatever the hell Dad calls them. I could more easily tell Mum. But I don't tell them anything about my weekends with Dad, and I'm not sure I understand why. No, that's not strictly true, I do partly get it. It's about protecting Dad, as if telling them we went to a burger joint or we watched movies or we hung around the shopping centre or we just laughed at stupid stuff, would be giving them tickets into that world. The world Dad and I have created. And I don't want to do that. It's ours. It's all we have. It's all we've been allowed since my parents got divorced. So maybe not just protecting Dad, but protecting me as well. I don't know. It's hard thinking about this kind of thing.

'Oh, you know. Stuff.'

Sam doesn't normally push. Like I said to Elise, he's so defensive about our relationship that it borders on the funny. But he gave a small shove.

'Stuff?'

'Yeah,' I said. 'Things.'

'Oh, things,' he said. 'I get it now.'

'Stuff, things and whatever,' I added.

'Wow,' he said, dipping a spoon into the pot on the stove and taking a sip. He frowned and reached for the salt. 'I can't compete with that level of excitement. You must be glad to get home and give your nervous system a chance to settle down.'

I smiled, put my school stuff away in my bag and started to set the table. Mum arrived ten minutes later, complaining about the parents who didn't show up at all, and the parents who did.

'You know, when I see their mums and dads, I understand why some of the kids I teach are the way they are. God, that smells good, Sam. What is it?'

'Bean ragu.' Mum is vegetarian, which means Sam and I, by default, tend to be as well.

'Don't care what it's been,' said Mum. 'What is it now?'

'Boom, drop mic,' said Sam.

'Stop being embarrassing, you two,' I said.

The ragu was good, the conversation okay and when all of it was over I went to my room to work on my short story. It *needed* work. But even as I lay on my stomach, pencil in my mouth, staring at the pages I'd already written, wondering if they really were any good at all, loud words from downstairs drifted towards me. Mum and Sam were keeping it as quiet as they could, but the noise wafted under my bedroom door nonetheless. I only caught a few words. 'London' was one. 'Opportunity' was another. 'Life-changing' might have been another.

But my name was definitely in the mix.

# CHAPTER THREE

★

'Do you want to read my short story?' I said to Elise. We sat at our normal places on a bench by the canteen.

'No,' said Elise.

'Are you sure?'

'Yup.'

I put the sheets down on the bench, being careful to avoid the damp patch from my water bottle. I figured you'd have to have a heart of stone to not be tempted by the words marching down each page.

'You might enjoy it,' I said.

'Unlikely.'

'Why?'

'Because I'm not going to read it.'

I sighed. 'Don't you care about my feelings at all?' I asked.

'Nope.'

'Surely you must be the tiniest bit curious?'

This time Elise sighed.

'I know what it'll be like,' she said. 'I mean, it's okay to be just, you know, shit-hot at English. A whiz kid with words. But no. You have to be a freaking genius.' She picked up her sandwich and pointed it at the sheets, then at me. 'It'll be brilliant and I have no reason to feel more inadequate than I do now. No wonder you've got no friends.'

'True,' I said. 'Friends are supportive and would read short stories that other friends have written.'

'Exactly,' she said. 'You've got no friends. Proves my point.'

I gave it up.

'How's the war zone at home?' I said.

She unscrewed the cap from her orange juice.

'It's hilarious,' she said. 'Now the D word is out there, it's all happiness and light. They are *so* nice to each other. And to me. It's like they're in some kind of reality TV show where everyone is disgustingly . . . freaking nice. Tell ya, I wish they'd always been unhappy. My childhood would've been brilliant.'

'I'll bet they talk a lot and don't say anything.'

'*Exactly*,' said Elise. 'That's exactly what they do. What idiots.'

'You're still in Phase 1,' I said. 'That's a good phase.'

'The others?'

'Oh,' I said. 'I wouldn't dream of pre-judging. But hey, kid. All I can say is strap yourself in, because it's a wild ride.'

'I hate you, CC,' said Elise.

'I know.'

As always when it's his turn to have me for the weekend, Dad picked me up after school on the Friday.

'What do you want to do this weekend, kiddo?' he said as I belted myself into the front seat.

'We could go in search of UFOs,' I said.

Dad put the car into gear and pulled out into traffic.

'We *could*,' he said. 'But you know what I reckon? I think UFOs are not the kind of thing you *can* go looking for. I think they'll find you when they're good and ready. When you least expect it.' He glanced over at me. 'Tell you what. You think about Saturday and Sunday. Tonight we'll go down to St Kilda beach, have a picnic. What do you say? We could get a takeaway pizza from Republica, watch the sunset, chew the fat or the margherita, whichever you prefer. Solve all the world's problems.'

'Solving all the world's problems seems like a great way to spend a Friday evening,' I replied. 'And the other good thing is once we get that out of the way, we've still got the weekend.'

'Atta girl,' said Dad.

It wasn't going to be a *spectacular* sunset. You can tell by the way the clouds ride the horizon. But the sun was pretty and fire-red as it kissed the sea. You could almost hear it hiss.

Dad and I had got a good spot and we sat eating and drinking and not really talking too much. It's one of the things I love about Dad. He knows when to shut up, when to keep his thoughts to himself and let others do the same. That's not to say he won't talk when I want to. And after I'd put away over half a large pizza, I suddenly wanted to.

'Dad?' I said.

'Hmmm?'

'Why have you never found another woman after Mum?'

Dad shifted himself onto his knees and faced me.

'What's to say I'm into women anymore?' he said. 'Maybe after the divorce I decided that men were the way to go. That's the problem with your generation, Cate. You're closed off to possibilities.'

'Okay,' I said. 'I am suitably ashamed. Let me rephrase. Why have you never found another partner after Mum?'

'What makes you think I haven't?'

I gave this some thought.

'Maybe because I've been staying with you every other weekend for seven years,' I said, 'and not once have I seen you with anyone else. It's always just the two of us.'

'That's a problem?'

'No, of course not.' I didn't really understand why I was having this conversation. I'd thought about Dad's apparent monastic existence plenty, but the time had never seemed right to bring it up. It didn't seem right now. Maybe it's like UFOs. Maybe sometimes conversations find you. 'But I worry about you, Dad. Sometimes I think that perhaps you'll grow old and lonely, that you'll never find someone to talk to about adult stuff or ... I don't know ... I don't like the idea that you'll never have someone to keep you warm in bed, no one to snuggle into, no one to tell you how wonderful you are, no one who will make your eyes light up when you see them.' I felt like crying and I didn't know why. Actually, I *did* know why. Dad took my hand in his.

'Answer me something, Cate,' he said. 'At what age do you think you'll be an adult? I don't mean when you can vote or drive a car or have sex or any of that stuff. When do you *feel* you will be an adult?'

'I don't know, Dad.' When I thought about it, it seemed like a question without an answer. You'd only know when it happened.

'I'm thinking sixteen,' he said. 'And I know that's arbitrary. Like, fifteen years and three hundred and sixty-four days you're a kid and then, bang, you wake up an adult.' He took a swig of his ginger beer and frowned. I knew he wanted a proper beer but you can't have alcohol on St Kilda beach. 'That's stupid. But I have to work with something.'

'Where's this going, Dad?'

'I want to give you my full attention while you're still a child, Cate. I don't want to share you with anyone else. For our weekends, it's just us. The rest of the time?' He shrugged. 'I work. I see people. Believe it or not, I go on dates.' He chuckled. 'My bed hasn't always been cold, you know.'

We both did the yeew thing together and then laughed.

'I like the world we've got, Cate,' he said. 'I don't want to share it. Not until you hit sixteen, at least. After that, who knows? Maybe I'll start introducing you to all the women who are throwing themselves at me in a frankly embarrassing and undignified fashion.'

I thought. It was good to know that Dad wasn't a hermit and I was glad I'd brought the subject up. Now I wouldn't have to do it again. Because we both liked the world we'd created. I didn't want to share it either.

'Excuse me?'

I looked up. Two young men stood in front of us but it was difficult to make out their faces. Maybe they weren't young men. They seemed more like boys, but their faces were sorta lost against the darkening sky. One of them carried a guitar.

'Are you Caitlyn Carson?'

I turned to Dad, who shrugged.

'Yes,' I said. 'Who are you?'

'Then this is for you,' said the one without the guitar.

And he started to sing. After a few words, the guy with the guitar started fingerpicking. It was a song I'd never heard before.

'*You fill up my senses, like a night in a forest. Like the mountains in springtime, like a walk in the rain. Like a storm in the desert, like a sleepy blue ocean, you fill up my senses. Come fill me again.*'

I so wanted to laugh, but another part of me wanted to cry. I could tell the song was way old, but it was . . . beautiful. So I just sat there. I wasn't even embarrassed, though everyone around must have been staring at us.

*'Come let me love you, let me give my life to you. Let me drown in your laughter, let me die in your arms. Let me lay down beside you, let me always be with you. Come let me love you, come love me again.'*

There was a couple of minutes more and, as far as I could tell, the lyrics just sort of repeated. It should have been silly, it should have been predictable, ludicrous, but it wasn't. I watched the young man sing. He gazed into my eyes and for a moment or two it felt like the words were only for me, that he *did* love me and wanted to drown in my laughter, die in my arms. God help me, I wanted it too. Maybe not the dying bit. I choked on laughter as I thought about it. How would I explain that to all the people here on St Kilda beach? *I don't know. One minute he was fine. The next, he drowned in my laughter and died in my arms. Should I have thrown him a lifejacket?*

It was over too soon. They finished the song, bowed and walked away. People around applauded. I nearly forgot to join in. To be honest, I was too emotional. No one had ever sung a song to me before, looked into my eyes and made me feel as if the words had been written for me and no one else. I had to choke back sobs. I was a mess.

When I had a bit of control, I turned to Dad.

'What was that about?' I said.

'You have an admirer,' he said. 'That much is obvious.'

'The song?' I knew he'd know it. It was old enough and so was he.

'"Annie's Song",' he said. 'John Denver. He wrote it for his wife, I don't know, sometime in the early 1970s.'

'For something so old, it's incredibly beautiful,' I said.

'Ah.' Dad drained his ginger beer, looked at the empty bottle as if it had disappointed him somehow. 'Yes. Old. Incompatible with beauty, normally, with just a few exceptions. Mozart, Beethoven, Bach. They didn't know about rap then, mind. The poor delusional fools. And as for words, well, old Shakespeare couldn't really string a sentence together. No idea of beauty, that man. Then there's Steinbeck and Hemingway and Emily Brontë, the old fools, and . . .'

I elbowed him in the side.

'Someone once said sarcasm is the lowest form of wit, Dad,' I said.

'Yes,' said Dad. 'But that was Oscar Wilde and he was *unbelievably* old.'

'That was so lovely,' I said. I stared up at the gathering stars and felt those words' truth as something solid and indisputable. Who were those guys? Why had they sought me out? It was a mystery, like the stars above us. I like stars. I like mystery. I smiled.

# CHAPTER FOUR

★

Later, I showed Dad my short story. He was the third person to read it, after Mum and Mr Carlisle, my English teacher. He sat on the sofa, beer in hand, my story in the other. I watched the television, its volume on really low. It was a program involving good-looking people, animated conversation and close-ups of faces soaked in various emotions. It was tiring just watching it, but better than having to put up with the dialogue, I guessed.

I avoided the temptation to glance over at Dad from time to time as he read. That's too *needy*. Why was I getting my parents to read it anyway? They were invested and therefore couldn't be trusted. I remember a teacher once told my class that he thought every newborn baby looked like a cross between Alfred Hitchcock and a bulldog (I had to google Hitchcock – and bulldogs, if I'm going to be honest) and that struck me as hilarious and profoundly true at the same time. And then he said that when his own kid was born he thought she was the most beautiful thing he had ever seen. That was eight years ago, he said, and when he looked back on the early photographs he realised she'd looked like a cross between Alfred Hitchcock and a bulldog.

Emotional investment. Can't be trusted.

Even Mr Carlisle had an axe to grind. I was his student, after all. When I asked him to look it over after class, he'd dutifully read it, took off his glasses and rubbed at his eyes.

'Well?' I asked.

My teacher sighed. 'It is . . .' I waited while he tried to find the word. 'Wonderful,' he finished. Then he held my gaze. 'And I don't use that word lightly, Caitlyn. It is full of wonder. It is ambitious, it is superbly well-written, it is surprising. To tell the truth, it made me want to cry.'

'Why?' This was great. Of course it was, but I needed more. I needed *reasons*. And the story wasn't overly emotional. At least, I didn't think it was.

Mr Carlisle thought for a moment.

'It's words,' he said. 'You know the way some people cry at the beauty of a song? I do that with words. Sometimes – not very often, but sometimes – a sentence can strike me as so . . . perfect that it brings a lump to my throat and tears to my eyes.' He laughed. 'And I can't stop it. Even when I know it's coming – when I'm teaching it for the thousandth time – it will ambush me. Did I ever teach the poem "Fern Hill" to your class?'

I didn't think so.

'It's by the Welsh poet Dylan Thomas and it finishes with the lines, "Time held me green and dying, though I sang in my chains, like the sea."' He laughed again and wiped at his eyes. 'It's done it to me again. For thirty years, ever since I discovered that poem, I've cried over those lines. Every single time.'

'What others?'

'Are you trying to make me into more of emotional basket case than I am already?' He held up his hands in mock horror. 'You're torturing me.' He thought. 'Lots of Shakespeare. The ending of Ian McEwan's *Atonement*. The line in William Golding's *Lord of the Flies* – "Ralph wept for the end of innocence, the darkness of man's heart, and the fall through the air of a true, wise friend called Piggy."'

The words caught in his throat and he smiled, but it came out kind of crooked.

'And my story made you feel like that?'

He got up from his chair and started to clean the whiteboard. It was the end of the day and we were all due to go home.

'Not all of it,' he said over his shoulder, 'but bits. Yes. You have this ability to take words that by themselves are unremarkable, but when put together, in a particular order, make music that moves me.' He turned to face me. 'Caitlyn, would you mind if I entered this into a short story competition? I'm a member of a local writers' group and we get news of national and local competitions. I'd like to enter this story in one competition I have in mind.

I'll get your parents' permission, of course, if it's okay with you.'

'It'll be okay with them, Mr Carlisle,' I replied. 'And it's certainly okay by me. Thank you. It's ... good to know that my writing has something going for it. Sometimes I think I can't write at all.'

'Then you really *are* a writer, Caitlyn,' said Mr Carlisle. 'All proper writers grapple with self-doubt on a daily basis.'

Dad put the last page down.

'This solves one question regarding genetics,' he said. I cocked my head. 'You get your creative abilities from your mother, that's for sure.'

'Stop it, Dad,' I said.

'It's okay. After all, you inherited my fabulous good looks, stunning sense of humour and modesty, which is a big plus if I say so myself. But your imagination ... well, I can't take any credit for that.'

'So you think it's good?'

Dad turned up the television volume. Someone with a face saturated in misery asked, 'But why, Joanne? Why would you do that to me?' Even over that I could hear Dad's reply.

'Stop fishing, Cate. You know it's good. To be honest, I'd like to say it wasn't, because you're getting to be a right pain in the arse. A talented pain in the arse, true, but one nonetheless. So shut up and listen to the dialogue in this soap. You might learn something about good writing.'

I didn't, but we had a good laugh.

★

Mum and Sam were lying in wait when Dad dropped me off on Sunday evening. We'd had a quiet weekend after the serenading on Friday night. Took in a movie on Sunday and had lunch I couldn't eat since I was stuffed full to bursting with popcorn. Even with not much on, Dad was still an hour and a half late dropping me off.

'Did you have a nice time, Cate?' asked Mum.

'Are you guys getting a divorce?' I asked. At least it stopped Mum's line of questioning. There was a shocked pause.

'We're not married,' said Sam.

I waved the objection away.

'That's small print,' I replied. 'Are we talking the big D?'

Mum glanced at Sam, Sam glanced at Mum. They both glanced at me. I waited.

'What makes you think that?' said Sam after a long time.

'Oh, I don't know,' I replied. 'My name drifting up the stairs and into my bedroom when you think I'm asleep. The way you look at each other when you believe I'm not looking. The fact you're both lying in wait for me with cheerful expressions and an agenda in your eyes. Tell me. Am I close?'

'No,' said Mum.

'Oh,' I replied. 'Well, that's good then. So are we going bankrupt?'

'What?'

'Loud words,' I pointed out. 'Affairs of the heart or money. One of the two. So does Sam have a secret gambling problem and is up to his ears in debt to a person called Luigi with a shiny suit and an entourage of guys built like brick toilets?'

Sam turned to Mum. 'Maybe we should get married, just so I can divorce you. Who needs a stepdaughter like this?'

'Are you proposing?' I said. 'How romantic.'

'We have not been arguing,' said Sam. 'Your mother and I have been having . . . *robust* discussions.'

'Sam has been offered a job in the UK,' said Mum.

That stopped me. Words rising through the darkness to my bedroom echoed in my head. *London. Life-changing. Cate. Cate. Cate.* I tried to work through the implications but they were . . . shadowy.

'What job?' I said finally. It wasn't the greatest question, but the best I could manage under the circumstances.

'An advertising agency in London,' said Sam. 'A good one. Actually, a world-leader.' Though Sam was a personal trainer when he and Mum met, he'd gone back to his original profession in advertising sometime after. I'd gathered, from occasional conversations on the subject, that he'd been trying for a career sea change, but the money in fitness was crap, so he'd rejoined the rat race.

Now, he spent his time coining jingles for breakfast cereals or investment banks.

'And you're going with him, Mum?' The thought struck me and I felt like an idiot for not having grasped it before. Then again I'd had less than two seconds to think all this through, so I suppose I shouldn't be hard on myself. 'You want *us* to go with him?'

'No, no.' Mum waved a hand as if the question was among the most stupid she had ever been asked. 'Well, yes. Maybe. We're talking about it, that's all.'

'I haven't accepted,' said Sam. 'It's a big move and needs careful consideration.'

I couldn't argue with that.

'So we just thought we should bring it out into the open,' said Sam. 'You know, talk it over as a family before making any decisions.'

'So why have you been arguing?' I asked. 'Sorry. Let me rephrase. Why have you been having "robust discussions" about it?' It seemed a reasonable question, but no one was apparently prepared to answer it. At least, not then.

# CHAPTER FIVE

★

'Oh my God, you're bullshitting me,' said Elise. 'What's the song again?' She was already punching stuff into her phone.

'"Annie's Song". John Denver.'

In twenty seconds, the song was playing through her phone. We listened for a while.

'It's not as romantic on your phone,' I said. 'But when two gorgeous guys are singing it to you under the stars, well . . .'

'So show me.'

'Ah. Slight problem there, Elise.'

She slapped the side of her head. Then she slapped the side of *my* head.

'You didn't take pictures?' she said. 'Videos? You know, like a freaking normal person would've done?' The last five words built in volume, so that the final syllable was a blast in my ear.

I think I might have mentioned that I hate Elise sometimes. That most times I love her.

'I know. I'm an idiot.'

'True that, CC.'

'But I didn't think. At the time I was too busy listening, you know?'

'You didn't think? True that, CC.'

Sometimes I think Elise and I are stuck in a conversational loop. We listened to the end of the song and Elise sighed.

'That's one of the shittest songs ever and the seventies produced more shit than any other decade.' She thought for a moment. 'Except the eighties and the nineties,' she added. 'And the noughties, obviously. But I would've died if someone had sung that to me. I hate you, CC.'

'I know.'

'So who? Who's got the hots for you? Dish some dirt.'

I knew. Of course I knew. But I wasn't going to tell Elise. Sometimes it's important to keep secrets, even from your best friend. So I told her about Sam's bombshell instead.

'You can't go,' she said, matter-of-factly, when I was done. 'Can't happen.'

'Why?'

'You'd be lost without me,' she replied. 'Come on, CC. Face facts. You're unpopular in school. No one likes you. Your teachers hate you. Even your parents think you're shit. I'm the only one who can put up with you, missy.' She reached over and patted my hand. 'So, you can't leave the one person who thinks you're okay, to travel to the other side of the world. No freaking way. Trust me on this.'

I wanted to laugh but it stuck in my throat when her mouth twisted and I saw tears in her eyes. They brimmed, but didn't overflow. It was like a punch to my gut. Elise put her head down, swallowed. When she looked up she gave me a smile, but I don't think it believed in itself. She clasped my hand in both of hers.

'Want to know something, CC?' she said.

'Of course,' I replied.

'I hate you,' she said.

'I thought you just said I was okay.'

She wiped at her eyes and the tears and the moment was gone.

'Nah,' she said. 'I'm with everyone else. You're shit.'

Mum took me out for a meal that evening. Just the two of us. That's when I knew it was serious.

'You really want to go, don't you, Mum?' I said over my chicken chow mein. I always use chopsticks, though perhaps the word 'use' is a stretch. I've put in hours of practice, I've even watched YouTube videos, God help me, but it makes no difference. The chopsticks slide over each other, catapulting noodles, lumps of chicken and the occasional slice of vegetable over the tablecloth, so I pick them up and put them back into the bowl. Caitlyn Carson *never* gives up. Sometimes I get a morsel of food near my mouth but it always drops down my front, making me seem like a six-month-old tackling her first solid food. In the end I get my mouth close to the bowl and use the chopsticks as a type of shovel. Apparently, that's often how the Chinese do it, but I still feel like a bogan.

'I wouldn't say that, Cate,' said Mum. She waved her chopsticks as if for emphasis. Mum is *great* with chopsticks, thus adding to my feelings of inadequacy. She picks up individual peas. Effortlessly. Sometimes I think she just does it to annoy me. 'It's an idea at this stage. That's all. But you have to admit it's an exciting idea.'

'London was like the Covid capital of the world for a time there, Mum,' I pointed out. 'So it's exciting if you want to play Russian roulette with pandemics.'

'Oh, come on, Cate,' said Mum. 'We're *all* living with it now. Most restrictions have been lifted, especially in the UK, so that's no longer a barrier. It's the new. . .'

I raised a hand.

'Please don't say the new normal, Mum,' I said, 'or I might have to pelt you with chicken chow mein.'

Mum smiled.

'Anyway,' she said, 'the virus is everywhere. But the Globe, Buckingham Palace, the Houses of Parliament, the Tower of London, Big Ben and Westminster Abbey aren't. Don't tell me you wouldn't be thrilled to see them.'

'What's wrong with Flinders Street Station, Federation Square and the Vic Market?' I asked.

'Ha ha.'

We ate for a while in silence. Well, Mum ate. I flicked stuff around.

'Fancy seeing you two here!'

It was Dad. He kind of hovered over our table as if unsure of a welcome. His smile seemed like it was coming undone around the edges.

'Sorry to interrupt,' he said. 'Just saw you, so I thought I should say hi.' He gestured over to a table in the corner. A woman sat there. She smiled when Dad pointed and then returned to her menu. I was thrilled. A woman! Dad on a date! I mean, he'd told me he went on them, but to be honest I'd found it hard to believe. I was desperate to go over and tell her that Dad was one of the world's best people and she should grab him, keep him, and not let him go. On reflection, I decided that would be scary and probably cause her to rush out and hail the nearest taxi, so I didn't. She looked nice, if you can judge a person from twenty metres away in half a second with a single glance. Which you can't. Obviously. Though I did.

'Hello, Mike,' said Mum. She smiled but I saw her glance over to the table as well. We'd both be checking out the mystery woman for the remainder of our meal. 'Good to see you.'

I got up and gave Dad a hug. A fragment of noodle transferred itself to his shirt, so I brushed it off. Then I hugged him again, but that was just a ruse so I could whisper in his ear. 'She's *hot*.' When I pulled away, he was blushing.

'Better get back,' said Dad. 'Enjoy your meal.'

After a couple of minutes, Mum sent them a bottle of wine just to show she was totally over Dad having a date, that she was cool with it, that generosity-of-spirit was her compound middle name. They both raised glasses to us when the waiter poured it for them and we mimed the same back.

Mum was the personification of grace. It didn't extend to her eyes, though. I can tell these things. So we continued the conversation, both pretending not to check out the couple in the corner at every available opportunity.

'So how long would Sam be going for, Mum?' I asked.

'It's not a question of Sam going,' Mum replied. 'As in, me staying here and him taking off. If I don't go, then he won't. Simple as that.'

I thought this over. On one level it was sweet. They were a proper couple, tied to each other. On another level it was disturbing. When we're bound to people it can be life-changing. It can mean the difference between shopping at Harrod's or the Vic Market. Strolling around the Tower of London or the Eureka Skydeck. And I knew I was bound up in this as well. Mum just hadn't played all her cards yet. It occurred to me that I might as well force them onto the table.

'If I don't go, what then, Mum?' I said. 'You won't go, so Sam won't go?'

The idea sounded terrible. Forever I would be the one who had ruined Sam's chances of making something of himself. I would have destroyed not just his career but possibly my mother's chance at happiness. How did I suddenly get such power? I didn't ask for it. I didn't want it.

'Well, I couldn't leave you here and go off to the other side of the world, could I, Cate?'

'You could,' I pointed out. 'I could live with Dad.'

'And what kind of mother would that make me?' Mum put down her chopsticks and rubbed at her brow, took a sip from her water glass. I thought that was a strange reply. *What kind of mother would it make her?* What about my feelings? Was it really important what judgements others might make about her parenting skills? Suddenly I wanted to go home. But this conversation was why we were toying with Chinese food in the first place. I felt I was making a mess of both. I couldn't grip the chicken or the words. They both lay scattered and messy around me. I tried to find some order.

'I would have to leave Dad,' I said. I tried to keep my voice quiet and reasonable. 'You didn't answer my question. How long would we all be going for?'

'I don't know,' said Mum. 'It's a permanent job, so . . .' She spread her arms.

'So possibly, probably, forever,' I said.

'Your dad could visit. We could send you back for holidays.'

'What kind of a father would that make him?' I said. Mum flushed, but I couldn't tell whether it was from anger or embarrassment. 'I have friends here,' I added.

'You'd make new friends.'

'I like my school.'

'You'd like another school.' Mum pushed her plate away. 'Cate, you're thirteen years old. You have your whole life ahead of you. You will almost certainly live in many different countries, meet more people than you can begin to imagine, make wonderful friends that right now you know nothing about. The love of your life might be there, waiting for you in London.'

I thought about a boy with a velvet voice. The love of your life could be anywhere. London. Louisiana. Lebanon. Of course, she was right. Moving to England would be a breathtaking experience. It would throw my life upside down, but maybe that's not such a bad thing. Maybe lives need to be thrown upside down from time to time. Maybe that's how we know we're alive.

Maybe, maybe, maybe.

But if my life was going to be thrown upside down, I needed to be the one to do it. Me. Not Mum, not Dad. Certainly not Sam and probably not Elise.

'I'll think about it, Mum,' I said.

She reached over and took my hand.

'That's all I ask,' she said.

'How long have I got?'

Mum frowned. 'The offer is on the table and apparently the company want him so badly they are prepared to wait some time for an answer. It's not a vacancy as such. It's more like he's being headhunted. But I guess even then there's a limit. So, I don't know. A month? Maybe two.'

I nodded.

'I'll think about it.'

'Holy shit,' said Elise. 'I thought I was the drama llama and here you are trying to beat me. It's pathetic. You need to grow up, CC.'

We sat in a corner of the library where students rarely go and where librarians turn a blind eye to kids chatting, provided the decibel level is incredibly low.

'Tell me about your drama,' I said. 'I'm tired of thinking about mine.'

'Mum's gone to a solicitor.'

'Uh oh.'

'They argue every night now.' Elise toyed with a lock of her hair. 'They wait till I'm in bed. It's almost funny. Again. They want me to piss off so they can stick knives into each other. And I'm going to bed earlier and earlier just to avoid the freaking . . . atmosphere. And when I'm up there I can still hear them, even though they're trying to be quiet.'

'What do you hear when you sneak out of your room and sit on the stairs?'

Elise gave me another of her looks. The *how do you know so much, smart-arse?* look.

'Money mostly,' she said. 'Mum wants to buy Dad out of the house. Dad wants to buy Mum out. They can't even agree what it's worth. Mum says if she buggered off she couldn't buy anywhere, once you take out all their debts. Dad says the same.'

'Is anyone using you as a weapon yet?' I asked.

'Oh, yeah. Mum says I'm staying with her, so she should keep the house to give me "continuity".' Elise made the quote marks in the air. 'Dad says that's so old fashioned and I should stay with him.'

'No one's asked you, though.' It wasn't a question.

'Course not. I just sit on the stairs while they talk *about* me. I'm a piece on the board and they keep moving me round. Is there a board game called *Divorce*? Should be.'

We sat for a while, mulling over our separate thoughts.

'I'm sick of being a freaking token in a game,' said Elise. 'But what can I do?'

I thought of all the responses I could give. Play them. If this is a game, then you have moves as well. One parent against another. Feign deep depression, so they stop arguing and focus on you. Throw things around. Fight at school. Get suspended. Steal a car. Cut yourself. But these weren't helpful. I shook my head. *Token in a game*? That pretty much summed up the pair of us.

'I don't know, El,' I said. 'All of this *will* pass. In the meantime, just look after yourself and call me whenever you want. Day or night. Literally any time. Call me.'

'What? Like at three in the morning?'

'Piss off! Are you crazy?' I put my arm around her shoulder. '*Any* time. You know that.'

We stayed that way for a couple of minutes and then Elise shuddered.

'Someone walk over your grave?' I asked.

'No. Don't know. Maybe. I just wondered what'd happen to me if you piss off to England,' said Elise. 'Can I tell you the truth, CC?'

'That depends on the truth,' I replied.

'I don't think I can get through this without you.'

I felt like crying, but instead I hugged her harder.

'What part of "depends" didn't you understand?' I asked.

My class had to do oral presentations. I gave mine on the Fermi paradox – the question of why, if aliens are all over the universe, haven't they showed up yet, other than to do stupid stunts in flying saucers in remote areas where a couple of bozos are gonna be amazed (thanks, Dad!).

I followed Elise, who gave her talk on the *Beethoven* film series. I know the *Beethoven* series because we watch some or all of them every time I sleep over at her place. And there are *eight* of the damn things. The first couple feature a Saint Bernard dog – the kind made famous by lurching through snow drifts in the mountains of Europe with a barrel of brandy around their necks, looking for people dying of hypothermia in the wilds. Or alcoholics who've got lost. Anyway, El *loves* those two movies, which is puzzling because El has a sensitive bullshit detector and the movies are kind of woeful. The dog, I have to admit, is so cute it's painful, but the stories are so corny it's even more painful. I've told her this on many occasions. *You wouldn't understand, CC,* she replies. *It's called having good taste.*

To be fair, it's not so much the movies she loves. It's the dog. She wants a Saint Bernard, but her parents laughed hysterically when she asked. So Elise is planning on leaving home when she's sixteen and getting an apartment and the dog. I worry about her grip on reality sometimes.

Anyway, it seems her enthusiasm for the subject wasn't shared by the rest of the class. There was silence when she finished.

I don't know how many of my fellow students enjoyed *my* presentation, but judging by the applause when I finished, at least some of them did.

I didn't mention the UAPs Dad and I had witnessed. Like I've said before: what happens on the visitation weekend stays on the visitation weekend. Though I make an exception for El, obviously.

I went back to Elise's place after school, partly because I wanted to stickybeak her domestic situation and partly to avoid mine.

I stared at the computer screen in her bedroom and tried to stop the contents of my stomach from making a dramatic appearance. Elise has a nice cream shag pile carpet in her bedroom and I didn't think projectile vomiting would improve its appearance. And why was I on the verge of throwing up? I read the opening paragraph on the screen again: *We understand how difficult it can be for new writers to have their voices heard by publishers, especially in the competitive world of writing for young adults and children. That is why we have our Book Pitch Program (BPP). It's very simple. Fill out the form below and then send us the first chapter of your book with a short synopsis (no more than 300 words) as separate Word documents. We guarantee that your writing will be read and if we are interested in helping you with publishing then we will be in contact within three weeks of you submitting your work.*

Elise nudged my arm. 'Go on then, ya bozo,' she said. 'Fill out the form.'

'I'm scared,' I said.

'Of a form?'

'Yes.'

'You're weird.'

'And what's your point?'

'Fill out the freaking form.'

The first field was straightforward enough. *Title of work*. I typed in *Unicorn Girl*. (I even put it in italics, to show how professional I could be. Was that professional? Would someone take one look at my title in italics and then immediately dump the whole lot in the recycle bin? I sighed.) Next field. *Author*. That was easy, though again I felt like throwing up. How could I put myself down as an author? An author is someone with a book in a shop or a library, not a thirteen-year-old with a Word file. I typed in *Caitlyn Carson*, then deleted it and typed in *Cate Carson*, then deleted it and typed in *CC Carson*, then deleted it. The blinking cursor seemed like a rebuke.

'Remembering your name's tricky, yeah,' said Elise. 'I can see why you're struggling.'

'Shut up,' I said. 'Which is better, El? Full name or Cate Carson or CC Carson? The last one sounds cool and authorish at least.'

'The last one's a lie. The last C in CC stands for Carson. What's the word when someone says the same thing twice?'

'Tautology.'

'That's it. How about C Tautology Carson? That is authorish.'

'Shut up, El.'

I typed in *Caitlyn Carson* again, moved to the next field. *Target audience age group*. I thought about it. *Birth to death and maybe beyond*, I wanted to write, but put down *ten to fourteen years of age* instead. Next. *Please provide a brief bio (a couple of lines about where you live and what you do)*. I was pleased with the brief bit. When you're thirteen it's difficult to get beyond a couple of lines. I put down: *I live just outside Melbourne, Victoria* (in case of the geographically challenged), *and I have a passionate interest in education, especially English Literature. I am currently working full-time in a school*. I skimmed the rest of the form. Nowhere did it ask for your age, which was a blessing (thirteen? – straight into the recycle bin) and I *was* working full-time in a school. Next. *What genre is your work? Despite the title*, I wrote, *this is realistic fiction*. Next. *Please summarise your story in one sentence (e.g. a love story involving young people from very different ethnic backgrounds/a fantasy about a girl with a magic power she doesn't understand/a story about someone travelling around Australia with his or her parents).* This was tricky. One sentence? Hmmm.

'How would you answer this, El?' I asked.

Elise slapped herself on the forehead. 'Hello, CC? I haven't read the freaking thing. I don't know what your novel is about because *you won't let me read it.* I'm allowed to read your short story, it seems, but not your book. If there's logic there, I can't find it.'

'Okay. A valid point,' I conceded. I chewed at my bottom lip for a minute or so, but that didn't help. Finally I wrote: *When a young girl sees a unicorn in a forest, she doesn't believe her eyes, yet that first experience of the miraculous sets her on a path to understanding that some things are just too wonderful* not *to be true.* I chewed my lip again as Elise read it over my shoulder.

'I'm trying for the mysterious,' I said.

'You've nailed the confused,' she said. 'What does that even mean?'

'You'd have to read the book.'

'You won't let me. Hello, CC?'

'A valid point.'

I read it over again. Maybe Elise was right, but I couldn't think of anything better. There was a box you could tick if you had any previous publishing history. I left it blank. I couldn't imagine listing my primary school magazine would have publishers scrambling to sign me up. Then it was simply a question of uploading the first chapter and the synopsis and pressing SEND. I think the first chapter had promise and I'd spent a lot of time over the synopsis. Both had been formatted properly and I'd rewritten that first chapter at least five times. I thought it was the best I could make it. One of the things I'd read in my research was that most first-time writers just send off the first draft and hope for the best. I wanted to polish mine so that a weary publishing eye might catch a glint of talent.

I read the disclaimer above the SEND button one more time: *You will receive an automatic email acknowledging receipt. If we are interested we will email you within three weeks. If you do not hear from us assume that we are not interested. No other communication will be entered into.*

'Here goes,' I said to Elise. 'Press send and throw my baby into the black hole of the publishing world.'

'You didn't put my email address down, did you?'

'No, my school email.' There was no way to distinguish, by the email address at least, a staff member from a student, so I thought that was safe. 'Not that it will matter, anyway, El. A no-reply is a no-reply whatever email you're using.'

'Wow,' said El. 'Miss glass-not-even-half-empty. Miss there's-nothing-in-the-freaking-glass-to-start-with.'

I pressed SEND.

'Your *baby*?' said Elise. 'You're such a mess, CC.'

Elise's parents were overjoyed to see me and positively thrilled to know that I was staying for dinner. They set to with a passion, smiling at each other over the kitchen central island and chopping, dicing and slicing with admirable cooperation. They hated each other, but for an untrained eye it was difficult to tell. It was also slightly unnerving, since they were both using sharp knives. I retreated to the front room where Elise was watching a quiz show on TV.

'Let's watch *Beethoven* after dinner,' said Elise.

'I would sooner have my front teeth extracted with red hot pliers,' I replied.

'I'll take that as a yes.'

'Thought you would.'

'Checked your school email yet?' said Elise, not looking up from the screen.

'No,' I said. 'I only sent it off twenty minutes ago.' I plopped myself down on the couch next to her. 'Well, once,' I added. 'Got the acknowledgment email.'

'What did it say?'

I ignored her.

The quiz show had entered the specialist round, where contestants answer questions on subjects of their choosing. One man was tackling questions on Victorian fungi. How do they find the people to set these types of questions? Judging by his answers there was only one person in Australia who knew everything about Victorian fungi and that was him. Did he set his own questions? I was going to ask Elise, but she already thinks I'm weird.

'If I go to London . . .' I said.

'You aren't.'

'If I go to London, then I will devastate Dad.'

'And me.'

'And you. And I will be devastated that you guys will be devastated as well as being devastated in my own right, having to leave you here.'

'Way too much devastation,' said Elise. 'You can't go.'

'But if I stay here, then Mum and Sam will be devastated, which will be devastating for me. If they go and I stay here with Dad, Mum will be devastated. So will I because I love my mum. Then again, I love my dad.'

'And me,' said Elise.

'Mostly,' I conceded. 'Though sometimes I hate you.'

'Damn it,' said Elise. She pointed an accusing finger at the TV screen. 'I *knew* that the lost fungus discovered in Ballarat in 2019 was *Phaeoclavulina abietina*.'

'So why didn't you say that?'

'Too obvious.'

'True that,' I said. 'So. Whatever I decide there will be devastation. I hate this, Elise. I really do.'

For the thousandth time I thought about the lack of control I had over my life. Sure, there were choices I could make but none that would please everyone. Especially me. It suddenly occurred to me that this was the reason I love writing. It's the only area of my life where no one can tell me what I should or shouldn't do.

'Seems to me there's one viewpoint you haven't thought about,' she replied. I opened my mouth but she beat me to it. 'Yours.' I opened my mouth again, but she was too quick. 'What do *you* want, CC? That's the only question here. Not your mum's feelings or your dad's – though, obviously, *my* feelings are way important – but what you want. It's your life and no one's gonna live it for you.' She pointed the remote at the TV and shut it off. 'Try not to think now, CC – shouldn't be hard for you – and just listen to your gut. Staying or going?'

I tried. I really tried, but the more I attempted to separate my feelings from my family's the more that seemed impossible.

'I don't know,' I said.

Elise sighed. 'Let's break it down. Pluses and minuses of Melbourne. Pluses first.'

'We have amazing fungi with unpronounceable names.'

'Oh, shut up, idiot,' she said.

And that ended the conversation. I didn't know whether to be sad or relieved. But I kept her question in my mind. What *did* I want to happen?

And then we went in for dinner where, it would seem, the world was a wonderful place and conflict was simply a dictionary word that everyone had forgotten existed. Well, *nearly* everyone. I could see pain in Elise's eyes, though she worked hard to hide it.

# CHAPTER SIX

★

Assembly is on a Tuesday every week. We have year-level assemblies on the grounds that Year Twelve students apparently believe that being in the same room as Year Eights is a shame beyond description and might necessitate ritual self-disembowelment.

That's fine for us Year Eights (not disembowelment, which is very messy if reports are to be believed), although it does mean you're more likely to be spotted by patrolling teachers if you're chatting to a friend. And it means we can be told about stuff that is specific to Year Eights, rather than having to listen to senior school pronouncements regarding university entrance. Not that we listen anyway, even to Year Eight–specific things.

Our assemblies are normally run by the year coordinator, but this Tuesday we were graced with the presence of the school principal, Ms Huddlestone. This meant we had to *pretend* to listen, which was somewhat annoying.

The year coordinator made some general remarks and then handed the lectern over to the Big Cheese herself. We sat cross-legged on the floor and tried to seem interested. She muttered something about academic excellence and the reputation of the school and then... she mentioned my name. At least, I think she mentioned my name. Judging by the way everyone turned to look at me, she *had* mentioned my name. I was stunned. Then she repeated herself.

'I would like Caitlyn Carson to join me on stage, please.'

What? I didn't want to join anyone on stage, let alone Ms Huddlestone, who had been known to reduce senior students to tears. Year Eights she chewed up and spat out for fun. What had I done wrong? I couldn't think. But my legs had obeyed a summons I wasn't even aware I'd issued. I stood and walked between the rows to the front of the hall. Then I looked at the steps leading to the stage. No way could I get up there. Not with legs made of rubber.

But the next minute, I was standing beside her. And the lectern. I looked down and rows of Year Eight faces gazed up at me. I got the strong feeling most were hoping I was about to be punished in ways beyond their wildest imaginings. Maybe disembowelment. But when I glanced up at the Enormous Cheddar I was relieved to see that she was smiling. I hadn't done something wrong. But I also couldn't remember anything I had done *right*. So I waited.

'Mr Carlisle, your English teacher,' she said, 'has let me know some very exciting news. Apparently, Caitlyn, you wrote a short story a while ago and Mr Carlisle entered it into a competition. And not just *any* competition. This is the Victorian Premier's Short Story Competition – an annual event that attracts high-quality entries by some of the best Australian writers. And I am delighted to tell you, Caitlyn, that your story won second prize in that competition. I should stress here, that this is not a competition limited to school-age writers, but to the best and finest throughout the country.' I was having difficulty absorbing all this. My face was burning and there was a rushing in my ears. 'The winner, I am told, is someone who has in the past been shortlisted for the Stella Prize – one of the most prestigious literary prizes in Australia.' She paused and looked down at me. 'And our very own Caitlyn Carson was runner-up.'

The Huge Haloumi placed a hand on my shoulder, which made me shudder. I didn't mean to; it was the shock. I really hoped she wasn't going to interpret that shudder as me finding her repulsive. I mean, I *do* find her a bit repulsive, but honestly – it was the shock. Anyway, she didn't seem to notice.

'Caitlyn has an invitation to attend an award ceremony in a few weeks' time, where she will be given a certificate and two thousand dollars in prize money by the Premier himself. I'd like us to show just how proud we are of her with a huge round of applause for our very own Caitlyn Carson.'

I was stunned four ways. I'd come second in a literary competition. I was going to meet the Premier of Victoria. The whole of Year Eight was applauding me as I made my unsteady way back to Elise. And *two thousand dollars*. I mustn't have heard right. It must have been two hundred. But even two hundred. Wow. It felt so good to have made money from writing. More than that. It felt miraculous. I sat down next to Elise, who put her arm around me. I kept my head down for the rest of the assembly and didn't hear another word that was said.

'Mr Carlisle?'

'Caitlyn.'

'I looked up the Victorian Premier's Short Story Competition on the internet and there is a fifty-dollar entry fee for each story.'

My English teacher looked at me over the rims of his glasses.

'I believe that's correct,' he said.

'You can't pay fifty dollars of your own money for my entry. That's not right.'

'Indeed,' said Mr Carlisle. 'Worse than not right. It would've been unprofessional. No, Caitlyn, I took your short story to the Head of English, she shared it with the faculty and we agreed to pay the entry fee from the English department's budget. The school paid, not me.'

'Well, I should pay the school back out of my winnings.'

'No, you shouldn't. That fifty bucks is a bargain when it comes to our bragging rights. Plus we want to publish it in the school magazine. Is that okay?'

I nodded. 'Of course.'

'Do you know who came third in the competition?'

I didn't. Mr Carlisle said a name, but it didn't mean a huge amount to me. I mean, I *think* I'd heard it before, but it's difficult to be sure. If someone *expects* you to find a name familiar it puts pressure on you to do exactly that.

'She was longlisted for the Booker Prize last year,' Mr Carlisle continued. 'Caitlyn, you beat a Booker Prize longlisted writer. Have you any idea what that says about *you* as a writer?'

'That the judges felt sorry for me because of my age?'

Mr Carlisle sighed, took off his glasses and rubbed at the bridge of his nose.

'The judges didn't know your age, Caitlyn. They didn't know your name. Your short story was a number only. That's standard procedure to ensure fairness in the judging process. Lay not that unflattering unction to your soul . . .'

'That's Shakespeare,' I said. 'Except he said "flattering".'

'Yes,' said Mr Carlisle. 'And he came fourth.'

I laughed even though it wasn't very funny. Teachers expect you to laugh at their jokes and it doesn't hurt anyone.

'You have enormous talent, Caitlyn,' said Mr Carlisle.

'And a remarkable imagination. Make sure you don't waste either.'

'I'll try,' I said.

Mum and Sam wanted to take me out for a meal to celebrate, but I liked the idea of staying at home, so Sam asked me what my favourite meal was and said he'd cook it for me. I went for spaghetti bolognese and he seemed a little disappointed.

'Are you sure, Cate?' he said. 'That's pretty basic stuff. I'm not a bad cook, if I say so myself, and I can do fancy.'

'Okay,' I said. 'I'll have lobster thermidor.'

'Spaghetti bolognese it is,' he said.

I'd tried ringing Dad during the day but he didn't answer, so I'd left a message. He rang me back while Sam was chopping onions and I retreated to my bedroom.

'Huge congo rats, Cate,' he said.

'Congo rats?'

'Why not? That is just brilliant. Tell me all about it. Go on. Run through the whole day.'

So I did. I told him about the announcement in assembly, that I'd won two thousand dollars (I'd looked it up – I *had* heard right), that I'd be attending a ceremony with the Premier, that of the top three writers, two were legends in the literary world and the other was just a leg end, that I felt . . . kind of giddy. I gave him the website address where he could find all the details.

'Do they know how old you are?' said Dad.

'Nope. The only thing they know is my name.'

'I want to be there when they see you. I want to see the jaws hitting the floors. I want to see my daughter make her entrance into the literary world. I want to see the expression on the Man Booker longlisted writer's face when she sees she was beaten by a scrawny, wimpy, tiny tacker.'

'Oi, Dad. That's me you're talking about, remember?'

'Can I be there, Cate? Are you allowed guests?'

'I don't know.' I didn't either. I hadn't even thought about it and the official invitation hadn't arrived yet.

Sam called through my bedroom door that the food was ready.

'Gotta go, Dad,' I said.

'Sure. You celebrate hard, okay? And then we'll do that all again on Friday when I see you.'

'Dad?'

'Yes?'

'Thank you.'

'For what?'

'For your belief and for . . . well, for my imagination.'

'Not sure I can take credit for your imagination. We talked about that, remember? Who knows how those genes fall?'

'I don't mean that. I mean for feeding it.'

There was silence for a beat or two.

'You are one weird, scrawny, wimpy tiny tacker,' said Dad. 'Now, pardon me but I'm due back in the real world right now. You should give it a visit sometime.'

And he hung up.

# CHAPTER SEVEN
★

A couple of evenings later there was a knock on the front door. It was bright and breezy (the knock, not the door), so I answered it immediately. I mean I would have answered it anyway, but . . . never mind.

Dad stood there, bright and breezy, a bunch of flowers in one hand, a bottle of wine in the other. He was such a surprise addition to our front doormat that my mind froze for a few moments.

'Dad,' I said.

'There's not a lot that gets past you, Cate,' said Dad.

'Dad,' I said, proving it wasn't just a lucky guess.

Mum's voice echoed down the hallway from the kitchen.

'Hi, Mike. Come on in. Be with you in a few minutes. Go straight into the front room.'

I shook my head in an effort to blow out the confusion there. It didn't work. 'I'll show you,' I said.

'I think I remember,' said Dad, squeezing past me and into the hall. 'It used to be *my* front room at one time. Well, ours.' He handed me the flowers and the wine. 'Better give those to your mother, get her to stick them in the fridge. Well, the wine, not the flowers. Though she can if she wants.'

'They're beautiful,' I said, burying my nose in the bunch.

'I know,' said Dad. 'I stole them from your front garden.'

'You did not.'

'You're right. I stole them from the supermarket.'

'What are you doing here, Dad?' I tried for a discreet whisper but I think it came out as a hiss.

'I accepted your mother's invitation for dinner.' Dad plopped himself into a chair in the front room and looked around as if to see what had changed in his seven-year absence. 'Didn't you know?'

I opened my mouth, then closed it again.

'I'll take these to Mum,' I said and beat a hasty retreat.

The kitchen was part-filled with smoke from the oven and steam from various pans bubbling away on the stove. Mum rushed around, stirring stuff and looking confused, dishevelled and slightly desperate.

'What is Dad doing here, Mum?' I asked.

'Can you check the pan with the broccoli in it, please, Cate? The nut loaf's got another half an hour and I want to get the vegetables ready.'

I stuck a fork into the bubbling green mass on the stove and it slid through the first floret with minimal resistance. The broccoli wasn't just done. It was done, dusted and fit for burial. In half an hour it would be a green puddle you'd have to eat with a soup spoon. Mum has many talents, but cooking isn't one of them. If Sam left, the pair of us would probably starve to death because I make Mum look like Jamie Oliver. I turned off the heat under the pan.

'All good,' I lied. 'What is Dad doing here?'

'I told you.'

'You didn't.'

'I did.'

I sighed and put my hands on my hips, but it was a wasted gesture since Mum was still bustling around her cooking disaster. So I put the wine in the fridge and found a vase for the flowers.

'Remind me,' I said. Mum *hadn't* mentioned it, but I knew there was no point in arguing. Then it hit me. It was so obvious, I should've seen it before. But then again, I had no idea he was coming for dinner. 'You want to talk to him about all of us going to England.'

'I told you that,' said Mum. I opened my mouth to say, *No, you didn't*, but shut it again. 'That's why,' Mum continued, 'Sam has gone out with some friends for the evening, so the three of us could have a good chat.'

'You told Dad about the England idea?'

'No.' Mum rinsed her hands in the sink and then relit the flame under the broccoli. I didn't say anything. There was nothing that could save them anyway. 'But I assumed you did. You know, him being your father and it being a life-changing decision and all.'

Even I had to admit it was a reasonable assumption. But I hadn't mentioned it to Dad and when I thought about it now, I reckoned it was for two reasons. Firstly, I believed I had at least a couple of months to mull things over, so there was no point talking it over with anyone (except Elise, of course). Secondly, it was a bit like the reason I didn't tell Mum and Sam about my weekend visits with Dad. What happened in the home, stayed in the home – theirs as well as Dad's. I like to keep things in their boxes. Was that my mistake or was that something my parents had nurtured in me? It was too difficult a question to consider.

'He has no idea why he's here,' I said. 'He's going to feel like he's walked into an ambush.'

'Oh my God, Caitlyn,' said Mum. 'I can't believe he doesn't know anything about this. Why would he have accepted my dinner invitation, if it wasn't to discuss you going to England?'

'I don't know, Mum,' I replied. 'Maybe he thought it was a generous offer, to spend some time as a family again, with no hard feelings. You know. Nothing on the agenda.'

Mum grabbed me by the arm.

'Go and tell him now, Cate,' she said. 'He can't be given this news over dinner. He needs *some* time to digest this.'

I had a feeling indigestion was going to be playing a large part in Dad's life over the next few days. Assuming he actually stayed for dinner, that is.

'Why don't *you* tell him?' I said. 'It was your idea.'

Mum put her hands on her hips and that wasn't a wasted gesture.

'It's not fair,' I said as I backed out of the kitchen.

'Life rarely is,' said Mum.

Dad sat up straight throughout my little speech, only swallowing a couple of times. It was like someone had snuck up behind him and smacked him on the back of the head with a baseball bat. He wasn't in this world but hadn't realised it yet.

'I haven't made up my mind, Dad,' I finished, then regretted it. It was like my words were a weapon hanging over him.

'Ah,' he said.

'I mean, there's lots to consider. Reasons to go, yeah. But reasons to stay as well. It's tricky. I mean . . .' I was talking too much. No, not talking. I was babbling. But Dad's silence was too big a void. I had to fill it, even with rubbish.

He made it to the end of dinner, though he didn't eat a great deal. Part of that must've been because the food was inedible, but it wasn't the whole story. He and Mum talked about the whole proposition, how it was a dream job for Sam, how Mum could easily pick up a teaching job in London from all she had heard. But mostly they talked about me and the amazing opportunities that Europe would present. I have to give Dad credit. He must've felt like the bottom was falling out of his world, but he was very reasonable, conceding that it would be a fantastic experience that few girls of my age could expect, that maybe they could discuss arrangements about him coming to visit or me flying back to Melbourne occasionally.

'Cate will be fourteen soon. I think that would be an okay age to travel by yourself,' said Mum. 'I mean, obviously Sam and I would see her onto the plane and you would be here to pick her up.'

Dad nodded and swirled some liquefied broccoli around his plate.

'Yes,' he said. 'That could work.'

There's reasonable and there's being so reasonable that it's unreasonable. I thought we were wading briskly into those waters. Maybe not wading. Plunging. So far, I'd sat opposite Dad and said nothing, mainly because no one had invited me to comment. I guess I could have jumped in, but I wanted to see how long they could talk about decisions that would turn my life upside down without ever asking for my opinion. Turns out that might have been forever.

So I just listened and fanned the flame of anger burning deep inside me.

I saw Dad out not long after the meal was over. Mum had offered him a glass of wine but he'd turned it down, partly because he was driving but mainly, I thought, because that would keep him there longer than necessary.

I left the front door ajar and walked him down to the car.

'Heavy stuff,' said Dad.

'None heavier,' I replied.

Dad jingled his car keys.

'You're angry that no one asked what you thought, Cate,' he said.

'And you're a mind-reader now?'

He chuckled.

'Oh, trust me, Cate. Your thoughts are always written on your face and in language that's impossible to misinterpret.'

'So why didn't you ask?'

'Sit with me in the car for a bit.'

He turned on the engine and put the heater on full. Within a minute or two it was toasty in the car.

'Think of the personal dynamics,' said Dad after a while. 'Your mum and I have an investment in staying reasonable with each other. It makes life easier for us, but it also makes things easier for you and that's something we both care passionately about.'

'Ignoring me is easier for me?'

'Let me finish.' Dad sighed. 'I could've argued. I could've presented another case where you staying here with me would be so much better. Europe can wait, continuing your education is important, unaccompanied flights across the world work just as well going to London from Melbourne as vice versa. You know that, Cate, because all those things will have occurred to you. Let's say I *had* done that. You would be in the middle yet again. Another conflict between parents and you feeling like a pawn in a game.'

Or a token.

'But . . .'

'And asking you your opinion around that dinner table would be forcing you into taking sides. Go or stay. In the end, that's what will have to be decided by all of us, but especially you. You *will* speak your mind to your mother. But when it's just the two of you. And you *will* speak your mind to me. Tomorrow, I hope, when it's just the two of us. What's the point in forcing you to make one of us feel bad back there? Divorced parents shouldn't witness one another's pain. We gave up that right when we split.'

I mulled this over, but I couldn't help thinking that, as always, he was being way too reasonable and fair.

'Speaking of pain,' I said finally, 'sorry about dinner.'

'It wasn't that bad.'

'You're right,' I said. 'It was worse. It was disgusting.'

Dad patted my shoulder. 'I do not necessarily agree with what you said, but I will defend, to my death, your right to say it.'

I opened the car door and stepped out into the cold of evening. Dad wound down the passenger window.

'Pick you up from school tomorrow, Cate.'

'Sure, Dad.'

'If I'm not in intensive care with food poisoning.'

'I do not necessarily agree with what you say, but I will defend . . .'

But Dad had driven off. I hugged myself against the

cold and went back up the front path to help Mum with the clearing up. And maybe to exchange a few unreasonable words.

★

'Cate, it's me.'

I resisted the urge to sigh. Even Dad must realise that his contact details would come up on my phone, but there was little point telling him again. Anyway, he sounded stressed.

'Have you left school yet?' he continued.

'Just about to.'

'Okay. Listen to me carefully because I will only say this once. Don't ask any questions, just do what I tell you to do. Do you understand?'

'Dad . . .'

'Do you understand?'

I sighed this time. 'Yes.'

'Okay. Leave by the back entrance to the school, the one on Griffith Street. Keep your head down and don't run. Across the road to your right you'll see a rental car. It's red and it has A1 Rentals on the passenger door. As quickly as you can, cross the road and get into the back of the car. Behind the passenger seat. Once you're in, crouch down in the well and I'll start driving. Whatever happens do not raise your head until I tell you it's safe. I'll explain everything when we've put some distance between us and them.'

'Dad. What the hell!'

'I know, Cate, and I'm sorry. But right now, I *need* you to follow instructions. I'm hanging up. Remember. Walk quickly but don't run.'

I tucked the phone into my backpack which I slung over a shoulder. *Head down. Walk quickly. Don't run. Whatever you do, don't run.* I'd seen enough TV crime series. They would notice someone running and we apparently couldn't afford to attract attention. Whatever story Dad was going to tell me, I knew it would involve people out there watching and waiting. So I had to be just another kid leaving school, blending into the general melee. Dad would explain what was going on once we were moving. (A rental car? Wouldn't that, in itself, attract attention? Who picks up their kid from school in a rental? I'd ask later – that seemed a design flaw to me.) I had a strong feeling he would be wearing some kind of disguise and my lip curled into an involuntary smile. But I squashed it as soon as it was born. Right at this moment, the situation was not a laughing matter. Yet.

I waited until a knot of kids left by the back gate and mingled in with them. I was in luck. They turned right and after a few steps I glanced up. The red rental car was across the road, lined up with other cars waiting for their children to come out. Ten metres of open road lay between me and the back door. Don't run. Don't attract attention. Make it seem like you are heading to the car behind and then jump in at the last moment. Should I wave? Would that seem normal, or would it attract the attention of someone scanning the mass of kids on the lookout for . . . well, for me? Too risky. It was important to keep the disbelief suspended.

It seemed to take forever but I finally had my hand on the door's handle. I opened it, slung my backpack in and then slid onto the seat and straight down into the well. At least it was clean down there and there wasn't any nasty smell. A decent rental company, then. I was grateful. But it was strange not wearing a seatbelt. That was so automatic I felt myself reaching for one before I remembered I was down on the floor.

Even before I'd settled, Dad had swung the car out onto the road and we were away. I could tell that he wasn't driving very fast, probably just below the forty-kilometre speed limit that marked out school zones.

'What kind of boring escape is this?' I said. 'I was expecting a roar of engine and the smell of burning rubber.'

'Not funny, Cate.' Dad's voice drifted down to me. 'Rule number one. Don't attract attention.' I couldn't help it. This time I snorted with laughter. 'Speaking of attracting attention,' he continued, 'you'll find a plastic bag on the floor next to you. There's a wig in there. Put it on and I'll pull over in a minute or two. Once I'm confident you won't be recognised, you can get into the passenger seat.'

I rummaged around and found the wig. It was blonde and would come down past my shoulders. This was fun. I couldn't wait to see what Dad was wearing. Given that he is someone with patches of hair just around and above his ears, with a skull that dazzles when the sun hits it, my money was on another wig. And if I was really lucky, a bushy moustache that curled down at the ends.

'What's the story, Dad?' I pulled my own hair back from my face, and pinned it at the nape of my neck.

'I'm so sorry to involve you in this,' he said, 'but there was no choice. I have a couple of rooms booked in a motel outside of town. Not in our names obviously, and I'll be paying cash. If it seems like we've thrown off the people chasing me, then we can go to a fast-food restaurant. Somewhere crowded where I can sit so I can see who's coming and going. We can talk through all of this then.'

'Yeah. Cool,' I said. The wig was a little scratchy and it had a strange, dusty smell, but it was a fairly decent fit and I couldn't wait to check myself out in the passenger mirror. 'But at least you can tell me who's after you. The mob? The police? Have you forgotten to take back your library books again?'

'Ha ha,' said Dad. 'But this is deadly serious. This . . .'

He never got to finish the sentence. Tucked up on the floor in the back of the car, I had no idea what was happening. Light filtered down from the windows but it only illuminated a patch of carpet. For all intents and purposes I was blind. But my other senses spoke. Loud and clear.

I'm not sure which was first, the sound of screeching tyres or the violent twisting of the car. There were all kinds of sensory inputs, though I couldn't make sense of them. The explosion of shattering glass, the wail of rending metal, the tumbling of fragmented light, someone screaming, though that might have been me, the smash of my head against something, the taste, bitter and metallic, of blood in my mouth, the smell of petrol, oh God, the smell of petrol and the realisation somewhere at the back of my aching head that petrol and fire were two sides of the same coin, the world turning over and over and the absurd image of me in a washing machine being spun into oblivion.

Full darkness did come. Eventually. When the world had stopped turning and the noise had changed to a sinister ticking. Then my body gave up. My last thought was that at least my wig was still on.

# CHAPTER EIGHT

★

The light was too bright. My eyes closed again. In the brief glimpse I'd got, the room was as white as the light. It was painful. No. Not the room. Me. *I* was pain. Then there was a face over me and some fumbling and mumbling of words that meant nothing, a pressure against my skin and the pain washed away, like a tide, leaving me gasping and struggling on some strange shore. The darkness returned and I embraced it. Nothing had ever felt as good as oblivion. I hoped it would stay forever.

The light came back. This time I remembered some things, but not all. Something about being in a car but not being able to see. An accident. Things twisting and tearing. Dad.

I wanted to sit up but I couldn't. Dad. What had happened to Dad? I tried to find some words but they were gone. My throat was clogged and it felt like my body didn't belong to me. I sent out instructions, but it ignored them. After a while I gave up, and my eyes closed on their own. Darkness was back. That was okay.

'Caitlyn? Can you hear me, Caitlyn?'

It was hard to resist the sound of my name. The light made me blink. Tears came to my eyes and made the white room blurry. There was a face again. It was a nurse. I knew that.

'Yes,' I said, but I'm not sure if the words were out there or just in my head, because her face disappeared. I waited. There was nothing else for me to do. It might have been a minute or an hour or a day, but then Mum's face was above me. She was smiling but crying at the same time. I thought that was puzzling.

'How are you, baby?' she said.

'Dad,' I said.

'He's okay,' said Mum. Even in my strange state of mind I thought she replied too quickly. 'You've been in an accident, but you're both okay.'

'I'm tired,' I said. Sleep was my friend. It felt like my only friend.

Our first proper conversation after the crash.

'You've been knocked around pretty badly, Caitlyn,' said Mum. This time I could see her properly. She sat on a chair at the side of my hospital bed. I was propped up, with what seemed like dozens of pillows under my back. The pain was still there, but it wasn't so . . . demanding. Now it just grumbled threats in the background, reminding me it still had teeth and claws and could use them. I couldn't trust it, but I knew I couldn't tell it to leave either. Not yet. Maybe not ever.

'What happened?'

'A car accident. A four-wheel drive T-boned the car you were in. The driver was well over the limit, both speed and alcohol.' Mum's face twisted in anger and then smoothed out. There were so many things, maybe wild and vicious, struggling beneath that surface, but she was keeping them chained up. For now. 'He walked away from the crash,' she continued. 'Of course he did. They had to cut you out.'

'Dad . . .' I said.

'They had to cut him out too, Caitlyn. He was in a very bad way. You should know that. And I'm only telling you now because the doctors are confident he will live, but for the longest time that didn't seem likely. You both survived a crash that by rights should have killed you. According to the police it was a miracle anyone came out of that wreck alive.'

The tears came during those last couple of sentences. No sobbing, just two streams running down her face. I'm not sure she even knew they were there. I thought about pointing out that maybe the miracle of my survival shouldn't be announced with tears, but I just reached out and took her hand. She gripped it so hard I had to bite my bottom lip.

'Can I see him?'

'Not yet, my baby. You're in no state to go to his room and vice versa. But he's down the corridor a couple of rooms away. For a week you were next to each other in intensive care.'

'A week?'

'You've been out of it a while.'

There were so many questions, but I couldn't grasp any of them. It probably didn't matter since the next time I opened my eyes, Mum was gone. Time was messing with my head. Everything was messing with my head.

'Elise.' I wanted to cry but I was too tired.

'CC, Drama Llama,' said Elise. 'Queen of soap operas. Well, you've done the big one this time.'

'Elise.'

Then we were both crying. A ridiculous snotty upheaval of tears and sobs, and we didn't care. She hugged me and the pain in the background growled but I didn't care about that either.

'Do you want to hear something funny?' asked Elise when we finally brought the mucus and tear juggernaut to a halt.

'More than anything,' I said.

'The word was you were going to die, CC. No one at school knew who said it first or if anyone said it at all.

But the rumours were all around. I talked to your mum. My mum talked to your mum. And she was nothing but, "Hey, it's all gonna be great," and she's smiling in the way that tells you she's really close to losing it. Like, this close.' Elise held up her thumb and forefinger so they were almost touching. 'And that told me she reckoned you were gonna die as well. So I prayed.'

'What?'

'I prayed. Every night, on my knees, next to my bed. I prayed you would live.' She wiped at her eyes and held my hand. 'You *ever* tell anyone about this and I'll kill you.'

I laughed so hard that it hurt.

'You bastard,' I said. 'I hate you.'

'I know.'

When I finally got control, I stated the obvious.

'Elise, you're an atheist.'

'I know. Told you it was funny.'

'So why did you pray?'

She shrugged. 'Passed the time. Anyway, it couldn't hurt. If she exists then she probably thought I'd be a convert. If she doesn't, then I was talking to myself. I do that all the time anyway.'

'So you're a convert now?'

Elise snorted. 'Nah. I'm a logical kinda girl. Science before superstition, that's what I say.'

'If God exists he's going to be really pissed off with you when it gets to Judgement Day.'

'If God exists, she'll be a she.'

'Why?'

'Because men aren't even close to being any freaking good. Look at our politicians, CC.'

'Okay. Then she's going to be pissed off.'

'She's all-forgiving is the word on the street. That's gotta help.'

'You are a mess,' I said.

'Takes one to know one, Drama Llama,' said Elise.

I gave her the update on my condition. Three broken ribs, a compound fracture of the femur and some internal bleeding, most of which wasn't life-threatening and was treated fairly easily. With the exception of the bleeding on the brain. That was the big one. Might have killed me. Might have left me brain dead. Elise opened her mouth to say something, but I beat her to it. Even *more* brain dead. Now it was a case of physiotherapy and monitoring the pain, mainly because the physiotherapy was going to hurt like hell.

Elise passed on messages from school. Apparently, I'd missed the big event for the Premier's award, so Mr Carlisle went on my behalf. It had been live streamed, so Elise showed me. The acceptance speech he made was really touching. He talked about how he had never known a kid with so much raw talent. He pointed out that I was thirteen years old, explained that I couldn't be there because of an accident. The next speaker said that if I could write like that at thirteen then no writer in the room, maybe in the state, maybe in the country, was safe, and they should all perhaps give up now. I found a few more tears when I was done watching. I couldn't believe I had any left.

I got to see Dad a couple of days later. A nurse stuck me in a wheelchair and took me to his room. I'd been warned that he was in an induced coma, so that his body could spend as much energy as possible repairing itself, but even so, the sight took my breath away. He'd lost so much weight and there were tubes up his nose and various things attached to every part of his body, or so it seemed. But it was the slackness of his face that shocked me. Almost like there was no one inside, that he'd slipped out of the room at some point and just left the furniture. The nurse assured me that was not so, that they expected Dad to recover. For all that, I wondered what would be left of him when that happened. I wanted to ask, but I was scared of the answer I might get, so I kept quiet. I held his hand and thought about praying. But I couldn't.

★

The conversation with Mum came the following day. I knew it was coming and I also knew that I could postpone it. Too tired. Too upset. There were a number of ways I could put it all off. But it was never going to disappear. I decided to deal with it early.

'Cate, I have a few questions I want to ask you.' She sat on a chair, Sam on another. I sat in a chair too, a blanket over my knees. Mum and I faced each other, like opposing counsel in some television courtroom drama.

'Go ahead,' I said.

'You were in the back of that car. A rental car, though no one's explained that to me. You weren't wearing a seatbelt when the crash happened, according to the police. Instead you were wearing a blonde wig.' Mum pinched the bridge of her nose, as if the words coming out of her mouth were so absurd that she was pained by their appearance. 'I would *very* much like an explanation, Cate. I mean, very much.'

'We were playing a game, Mum.' I didn't know how else to explain it. *Game* wasn't the right word, but it would have to do for now.

'A game?' Mum said the word like its meaning was a mystery. 'You were playing a game?'

'We play every weekend I'm with Dad.'

Mum rubbed at her forehead, pushing her hair back. Her eyes were screwed up.

'I don't understand,' she said. 'What kind of a game involves you being in the back of a rental car without a seatbelt and wearing a wig?'

Sam leaned over and put a hand on Mum's knee.

'Maybe we should leave this conversation for a while, Lois,' he said. 'Until Caitlyn's feeling . . .'

'What kind of a game?' she said.

I wished Mum had listened to Sam. Like I said, I wasn't in the mood for this; I was *never* going to be in the mood for this. But Mum needed answers. She's insistent and doesn't take kindly to being ignored.

How to explain? That Dad tried every time I was staying with him to bring some magic into my life, to arrange events to feed my imagination, to bring wonder and playfulness into what is an otherwise predictable existence? This was something between Dad and me. It was our secret, one I hadn't even shared with Elise. Yeah, I'd told her about the adventures, but not the explanation behind them. Hell, even Dad and I hadn't ever talked about it. We both knew the other knew, but we lived the lives and experiences he created and we believed. That was the key. Fiction isn't fiction if you believe in it enough. It becomes real. That's the key to this type of magic.

I couldn't explain this to Mum.

'We role-play,' I said. 'I think Dad had some kind of spy game in mind. He was just about to pull over so I could get in the front seat when the accident happened.'

'Spy game?' Mum's face was filling with anger. I was making a mess of my explanation. It sounded stupid, even to me.

'People were following us . . .' I thought about what Dad had said when I got in the well of the car. He'd booked motel rooms in different names, was going to pay by cash, take me to a fast-food place where he would stare at the door while he told me some story about . . . I don't know. Maybe he'd stumbled across a crime scene and now the killers were trying to silence him. Maybe he'd unearthed a terror plot and a hit man was coming for him. Maybe . . . It didn't matter. Dad would have a story and it would be fun. Perhaps, after we'd finished eating, Dad would suddenly say that we had to leave, that someone had spotted us from outside and our only chance now was to run. And we'd sprint through the streets until we got back to the motel and . . .

I realised I'd lapsed into silence.

'We make worlds,' I said. 'And then we live in them for the weekend. Or part of it, at least.'

'A spy game,' said Mum. She stood up and I realised that I had never seen her so angry. 'When you go to your dad's house you play games. Well, how fabulous, Caitlyn. How absolutely fabulous. While Sam and I bring you up, being boring caregivers . . . you know, cooking and cleaning and nagging you about school and cleaning your bedroom . . .'

'Lois . . .' But Sam might as well have asked the wind to stop blowing. Mum was beyond anyone's control.

'. . . your father is playing games. Being the fun dad. No wonder you prefer him to me . . .'

'Mum . . .' This was not true. Was it? I couldn't think about it because Mum's army of words was attacking without mercy and I felt surrounded and helpless.

'. . . and maybe that would be okay. Maybe it would. While we deal with the real world and all the shitty things that go on in it, you can escape into your stories . . . your *games*. Fine. Happy for you. But not this, Caitlyn. Not this. Your father put you into the back of a car and you were not wearing a seatbelt. I mean . . .' Mum laughed, but it was a strange thing, more like a squeal. 'I mean, parents are supposed to be doing that. Making *sure* you put on your seatbelt. You know why? Because they are there to protect you. But your father. He put you at risk.' The words were getting mangled now because her tears and her rage were building. 'For a game. He gambled with your life for a game. It's not right, Caitlyn. It's not right and I will never forgive him for it. I will never forgive him for it . . .'

And then she was gone, but I could hear her cries as she ran down the hospital corridor. She sounded like something trapped and howling in pain. I looked at Sam. Then I was aware of a tear dropping from my chin and onto my gown. I couldn't remember when I'd started crying.

'She'll get over it,' said Sam. He patted my hand but then withdrew like he had no right to touch me. Or maybe it was fear that, like a cornered animal, I might strike out. 'She's angry now, but she loves you.'

'I know.'

He gestured towards the door.

'I'd better . . .'

'Yes,' I said.

He smiled, but it was crooked and unrealistic. A small step towards me, a shuffle back. And then he was gone too, and I was left alone in the white room.

For a few absurd moments I wondered if Dad would appear at the door, tell me he was particularly proud of this little fiction but it was done now, the weekend was over and he'd drive me back to the real world.

That would've been wonderful.

# CHAPTER NINE

★

Elise brought me my school laptop the next day and I checked my emails. Dozens and dozens of them, all boring.

Except one.

*janebr@blakemcdonaldpublishers.com.au*
*Dear Caitlyn Carson,*
*Thank you for your submission of* Unicorn Girl *through our Book Pitch Program. I would much appreciate it if you would send through the complete manuscript for our consideration. Please understand that it takes on average about three months for an appraisal, so do not become discouraged when you do not hear from us immediately. Please also understand that this request for the entire manuscript does not mean an offer of publication.*

*We look forward to reading your work and will be in contact in due course.*

*Best wishes,*
*Jane Brown*
*Commissioning Editor*
*Blake McDonald Publishing House*

'Oh my God,' said Elise. 'You're gonna be the next JK Rowling. Will you still love me when you're famous?'

'Shut up, Elise,' I said. 'I don't love you now.'

'Yeah, you do.'

She said other things but, to be honest, I was too excited to pay much attention. They wanted the complete manuscript! Yes, okay. That didn't mean they were going to publish it. They made that point very clear in the email. But they also didn't say they *weren't* going to publish it. I was entitled to some excitement.

'This email is dated nearly two weeks ago, Elise,' I said. 'You don't think they'll have just given up? I mean, if I can't be bothered to send it, why should they bother . . .'

'Oh, now *you* shut up, CC. Just send it to them. Explain you've been knocking on death's door and that kept you kinda busy because you were waiting for death to answer.'

Luckily I kept a copy of the book on my school laptop, so I attached it to my reply.

*caitlyncarson@brineleessc.vic.edu.au*
*Dear Jane,*
*Please find attached the complete manuscript of* Unicorn Girl. *I apologise for the delay in replying to your email, but I have recently been in hospital*

*following an accident. I hope you enjoy my story and look forward to hearing from you in due course.*
*Best wishes,*
*Caitlyn Carson*
*PS: You might be interested to know that I recently came second in the Victorian Premier's Short Story Competition. I got this news recently, so wasn't able to put it into my original BPP application.*

'You don't think I sound too up myself with that PS, do you, El?'

'It's a business, CC,' said Elise. 'You'd be a bozo *not* to mention it.'

I read the email over about ten times, thought about changing some phrases, did so, then changed them back again. Eventually, Elise leaned over and clicked SEND.

'This Jane Brown'll be dead by the time you finish pissing about with that email,' she pointed out.

I let out a huge sigh. She was right. I worry too much about stuff like that.

I got a reply almost immediately.

*janebr@blakemcdonaldpublishers.com.au*
*Dear Caitlyn,*
*Sorry to hear about your hospitalisation. I hope you are fully recovered. Thank you for the ms and congratulations on your success in the Premier's Short Story Competition.*
*Best,*
*Jane*

'She called you Caitlyn and not Caitlyn Carson and she signed it with "Best", not "Best wishes",' said Elise. 'You're like close friends already. Hey, can I tag along with you on your international book-signing tour?'

'Shut up, Elise,' I said.

'Okay,' she said. 'Let's watch *Beethoven's 2nd* on your laptop. Then I'll shut up.'

'Shut up, Elise,' I said.

I was able to visit Dad every day, but they told me I couldn't stay for more than ten minutes.

'He knows you're here, love,' said one of the nurses when I asked why. Dad was still in an induced coma and he'd never once shown signs of waking up. I didn't understand why my being there could hurt him. 'We've got him on all kinds of drugs, but he's aware of some things. I don't know. It's a bit of a mystery, but I've seen it loads of times. See the way his eyes are flickering slightly under his lids? He senses your presence and he wants to wake up. That's why you can't stay long. He really needs his rest.'

So I stayed for ten minutes and held his hand and watched for when his eyes started twitching under his lids. As soon as that happened I kissed his cheek and went back to my room. Mum visited me (and Dad) all the time. Sometimes she had Sam with her, sometimes she came alone. We didn't talk about our argument, but I could tell by her eyes that she hadn't forgotten and probably hadn't forgiven. We would be talking about it again. But not now.

I was learning to read *both* my parents' eyes.

Finally, they let me leave. I'd been in hospital for four weeks and I was getting seriously claustrophobic. Sure, for the last week I was able to walk around the place, even visit the cafeteria for a while, though all of that tended to wear me out and I was often glad to get back to my bed, nursing a small pain in the leg that had been broken. But I was so relieved when the doctor finally gave me permission to be discharged. She told me I would have to come back twice a week for the physiotherapist to check on my progress and make sure I was still doing my exercises. That seemed a small price to pay.

My ribs sometimes hurt like hell. Apparently, they'd healed well. Normally it's six to eight weeks or even longer before they're back to normal, but youth was on my side. The doctor warned me I would still be uncomfortable for a while yet. My broken leg was coming along fine, though it would be at least another four months before it completely healed. Nonetheless, I could've walked down to the car park, but that apparently wasn't allowed, so a nurse pushed me in a wheelchair to the front doors and wished me luck.

I had the window open for the entire drive home as I listened to Mum chattering on about work and how understanding the school had been while I was in hospital. I put my head slightly out of the window and let the cool air blow hair from my face. At least I did until

Mum told me to stop. I think she had visions of my head colliding with a pole or something. I suspect having your daughter nearly die makes you slightly over-protective. So I just watched as the roads and buildings slid by and felt happy. Happy for that air on my face, the clouds scudding overhead, the words in my ears and the faint steady beating of my heart. A few moments of madness had nearly taken all that away. Yes, my father was in an induced coma, but I felt grateful for the simple fact he was still alive.

I wasn't allowed to stay over at Elise's. When I asked, Mum nearly had a panic attack. But my friend was allowed to stay over at my house, which was cool. We watched movies and she filled me in on all the gossip at school, of which there was plenty. She also confided that while I had been in the hospital, she'd got herself a boyfriend.

'Oh my God,' I said. 'Who is it?'

'Liam,' she said. 'Liam Cooper.'

I knew Liam Cooper. He was in the year above us and obviously fancied himself as really good looking. In a few years he'd doubtless sport a man bun and long sideburns and be the founder member of his own fan club. He was kind of revolting in an attractive way.

'How did you manage to get Liam Cooper as your boyfriend?'

'Oh, he doesn't know he's my boyfriend,' said Elise. 'Yet.' She scrolled through her phone for a while. 'I might tell him in a day or so. I think he probably needs to know.'

'But . . .'

'If you're going to piss off to the other side of the world, then I reckon I deserve a boyfriend. I've decided on Liam.'

'I can't see me going,' I said. 'And I can't even think about it with Dad the way he is.'

'Good,' said Elise. 'Music to my ears. If you stay I'll probably dump Liam as my boyfriend so I can focus on you.'

'That is weird.'

'It'll break his heart, but what can you do?'

'You're a mess,' I said.

'Takes one to know one, CC,' said El.

Mum and I went in the day they brought Dad out of his induced coma. I hadn't even known they were going to do it, but found out later that they kept the information from me in case he wasn't . . . okay when he regained consciousness. According to his doctor, the intracranial pressure had come down to almost normal levels, so they had withdrawn the cocktail of barbiturates and brought him back slowly into the world. He had been confused at first, the specialist told us in his office, but was improving with every minute that passed. He had some memories of the accident, but they were incomplete. At the moment there was no sign of brain damage, but that could only be properly assessed over time. We were to spend no more than fifteen minutes with him today – less if he became agitated or overly emotional.

We tried not to cry when we went into his room, but it was one of the most difficult things I've ever attempted. Now that he was out of the bandages he looked... wrecked. It was like someone had jumped him in a dark alley and beaten the living daylights out of him. His eyes were sunken, with huge bags under them, and there were lines on his face I swear weren't there before. He had aged fifteen years in a few weeks. He gave a small smile when he saw us, but even that appeared to exhaust him.

'Hi,' he said in a voice barely more than a whisper.

'Dad,' I said.

'There's not a lot that gets past...' but he coughed before he could finish and that exhausted him even more.

We spent just five minutes with him that first day and we didn't say very much. Dad just stared at me with those sunken eyes and I held his hand. When his eyes closed and his breathing settled into a rhythm, Mum and I left.

It was only when we were in the corridor that we cried. That was messy as well. All my recent crying had been messy.

Sam made spaghetti bolognese with his home-made garlic bread. He did a vego version for Mum. It was delicious, but even as we were eating I knew that something momentous had appeared on our mental horizons.

The realisation made me scared. At least I didn't have to wait long.

'Sam is flying to England in a week's time,' said Mum. 'The company were putting pressure on and . . . well, he's made his decision. It's too good an opportunity to miss.'

'Oh,' I said. There were other questions, of course, other factors, but we'd get around to those. 'Congratulations,' I added.

'I'm staying here, of course,' Mum continued. 'You are in no fit state to travel that kind of distance, so that's a no-brainer. Plus, we couldn't possibly leave until both you and your father have made further progress with your recoveries.'

'Yes,' I said.

'But you should know, Caitlyn, that I intend to join Sam in England as soon as humanly possible and that you will be coming with me.'

I hung my head. The spaghetti was no longer delicious. The garlic bread was a pale lump on my plate. I swallowed a couple of times.

What could I say? I could argue. I could ask how we had come from a position of talking about moving, with me apparently having some say in the matter – you know, a semblance of control over my own destiny – to a point where everything was decided, without me having said a word. My father was going to be left in Australia, sick and heartbroken, maybe never to recover fully. He'd have no say in the matter either. Mum was going to rip up my life, tear me away from my friends and my father because she was in love with someone who had nothing to do with me. Nothing. I hadn't chosen him. He was all right, but I hadn't chosen him. But now I was tied to him because of my mother's infatuation. Tethered to the extent that when he went to the other side of the world, we were both dragged after him. Like possessions, another couple of pieces of baggage that had to be checked through customs. I could have said that maybe Dad would have some legal ways to fight this. That I might have some legal ways to fight this. It was unfair to hit me with this so soon after such a terrible accident. I was hurting and now she was making me hurt more.

But I didn't say anything. I excused myself and said I was going to bed. And that's what I did, after throwing up some spaghetti bolognese into the toilet. But I didn't sleep. I didn't cry either.

Maybe tears had deserted me as well. That was good. I was sick to death of crying.

Sam talked to me the next day. Mum had gone to school and he had put in his notice at the advertising agency in the centre of Melbourne. They'd told him not to bother coming in again. Advertising has its eyes on the long term, it seems, so there was no point in Sam getting involved in projects he wouldn't be seeing through. He cooked me a big breakfast, but I knew I wouldn't eat much of it.

'I'm sorry about all this, Caitlyn,' he said after I'd pushed scrambled eggs around my plate for a while. 'I really am.'

Now here's a strange thing. I wasn't angry at Sam, I was angry at Mum. I mean, he was the one who was responsible for all this. If he didn't exist we wouldn't even be *thinking* about England. But all this was about Mum's choices, not his. Anyway, I like Sam. I always have.

'I know,' I said. 'It's not your fault.'

He sat opposite me at the dining table.

'That's good of you to say,' he said. 'But it certainly feels like my fault. It's *my* job in England. *My* acceptance. *My* decision to move. You must feel like you have no control. That's why I'm sorry.'

I pushed my eggs around some more. He'd summarised beautifully what I felt, so there didn't seem much point in adding anything. My silence would be eloquence enough.

'But there are things you should know, Cate.' He tapped his fingers on the tabletop, kept his head down. 'Your mother made it sound like it's her decision and her decision only. But that's not true. Your father would have to give his permission for you to move to England. Did you know that?'

'I suspected it.'

'Well, you're right. It's against the law for your mother to take you out of Australia permanently if your father hasn't agreed. Will he agree, do you think?'

I gave this some thought. On the one hand, I knew that Dad lived for my visits. Yeah, he said that he had a social life, that when I wasn't seeing him he led a normal existence, even going on dates. (I didn't want to think too carefully about how those dates were set up. Was his picture up on some sad dating app? I shuddered and tried to banish the image.) I had no reason to disbelieve him. But when we were together, I was the centre of his world. He'd made that clear and I had no reason to disbelieve that either. From the end of school on Friday right through to the time when he dropped me off at home on the Sunday evening, it was just the two of us. No one else existed. No one.

So, he'd do anything to keep me close. But I knew he also had my best interests at heart. How would he view me living on the other side of the world from an objective point of view? I had some evidence of his thoughts from that dinner conversation with Mum. I would have a wonderful time in England. New opportunities would arise. I could become a more rounded person through the experience. Would he agree to let me go because, although he loved me, he would feel obliged to set me free? *Because* he loved me, would he be obliged to set me free? In short, would he sacrifice his own happiness if he felt it was for my benefit? Oh, yeah. In a heartbeat. But he also would want to know how I felt. He wouldn't assume that my happiness was something that could happen against my wishes. God, this was all too confusing . . .

'I don't know,' I said finally. 'Maybe.'

*Good work, Caitlyn*, I thought. *You have a mind like a steel trap.*

'If he doesn't,' said Sam, 'then your mother will probably apply to court to get a judgement allowing her to take you out of the country.'

I gave up on the eggs. They just weren't worth it, so I pushed my plate away.

'That court,' Sam continued, 'will decide what's going to happen based on what is in *your* best interests. Not your mum's, not your dad's. But arguments will be presented, for and against, probably by lawyers. A judgement will be made taking into account a number of factors, one of which will be the histories of both parents.' He took my plate, scraped the leftovers into a bin and stacked the dishwasher. It took a few moments for the penny to drop.

Dad had put me into the well of a car. He hadn't made sure I was wearing a seatbelt. In fact he'd made sure I *couldn't* be wearing a seatbelt. And why? For a game. No matter how you argued it, Dad couldn't be presented as a responsible carer. Mum hadn't ever put me in danger. Dad had nearly got me killed. It was a weapon Mum would use. Of course she would. I didn't know how Dad could defend himself against that. Maybe he wouldn't want to. I had a sudden image of a judge in a powdered wig, listening to the account of the accident and gazing at Dad, his hand already closing on the gavel to give judgement.

'The reason I mention all this,' said Sam as he closed the dishwasher door, 'is to give you and your father time to think. And maybe prepare for everything that might happen.'

I got up from my seat and gave him a hug. He seemed surprised and for a few moments he didn't put his arms around me and return it. Then he did and I was glad, even though a small flame in my ribs flared briefly. It was the first time we'd hugged. Ever.

'You are a nice person, Sam,' I said as we broke apart. 'And my mother is lucky to have you.'

He laughed. 'Try telling her that. It seems *you* don't blame me for England, but sometimes I think she does.' Then his eyes changed, like he'd thought about what he'd just said and decided it was a mistake, that maybe he'd been disloyal to her. 'That was just a joke,' he added.

'You really love her, don't you?' I said.

'Oh, yes,' he said. 'Very much. And, if I'm being honest, more than anything else I want the three of us to be starting a new life together in the UK, as a family. There. I've said it.'

I went back to school four days later. There was only a week until the school holidays, so it was decided I would have time to recover then and a week shouldn't make me too tired. Plus, I was falling behind with my work and although the teachers would give me whatever time I needed to catch up, I wanted to get back into things. And I missed people. Especially Elise.

We sat together at lunchtime, as always.

'Update time,' I said. 'Two things. How's it going with Liam and how's the war zone we call home?'

'Ah, Liam,' she said. 'That poor guy. He's got it so bad. I don't think I've ever known anyone so head over heels in love.'

'With himself?' He'd always given me that impression.

'Ha ha. No. With me, of course. It's pathetic, really, the way he behaves around me, all puppy dog and pining away. Bit sad, to tell the truth.'

I took a bite of an egg sandwich. Why do they put a small amount of egg and a couple of cos lettuces between two slices of white bread? They should call it a *lettuce with trace amounts of egg* sandwich.

'Evidence please, Elise,' I said.

'Yesterday . . . you won't believe this. I was watching him play basketball . . .'

'I can believe that.'

'. . . and he was running up and down and not once, *not once*, did he even glance in my direction. I mean, that's freaking embarrassing. You know, *if I look over, then I will probably faint cos that Elise Carmichael's so gorgeous, so I'd better pretend to be right into the basketball.*'

'So he didn't look at you?'

Elise laughed. 'I know. It was so obvious it was hilarious. When they stopped playing, he even walked right past me like I was invisible.'

I whistled. 'He does have it bad, doesn't he?'

'I have him wound round my little finger,' said Elise.

'It's good to know your love life is thriving,' I said. 'What about the home front?'

Elise picked up the other half of my lettuce sandwich, opened up the slices of bread and picked out the green stuff, dropping leaves onto the ground. Then she reconstituted the sandwich and took a bite. I glanced down at the pile of lettuce on the concrete. So did Elise.

'Biodegradable,' she said. Then she sighed, picked up the mess and put it back into the plastic case that had housed the sandwich. 'They've started splitting things up,' she continued. 'If it wasn't so crap it would be funny. They were going through ornaments, for Christ's sake, deciding who was going to get what. I mean, there's stuff there the Salvos would throw out because it's so . . . shit.' She finished the sandwich and wiped crumbs from her mouth. I hoped she'd enjoyed half of my sandwich. I'd been looking forward to eating it myself. 'And they were arguing over this freaking vase. I mean, it's shit. Neither of them want it, they just don't want the other one to have it. So I picked it up, took it outside and smashed it on the floor.'

'How did that go down?'

'Very funny, CC. "How did that go down?" Yeah, anyway, I went back in and said, "There you go. Problem solved. Don't thank me." Then I went to my room and stayed there for the rest of the evening.'

'I'm so sorry, El.'

'Not your fault, CC, unless I missed a meeting.'

There were the tears again, catching glints from the sun, but not finding their way to her cheeks. She swallowed.

'Thank God you've got Liam, is all I can say.' I had to say *something*.

El gave a weak smile.

'I might have to dump him,' she said. 'He's getting way too needy.'

# CHAPTER TEN

★

Dad was getting better, but so slowly.

He was able to sit in a chair now, though not for huge amounts of time. He'd damaged some vertebrae in the accident, though the doctors told him he should have full mobility in the long term. According to Dad, a crack a few millimetres on either side and he'd be in a wheelchair for the rest of his life. I didn't tell him that the guy who'd T-boned us had just come out of his court case. Two thousand dollar fine, banned from driving for a year and a two-year good behaviour bond. Mum had had a few words to say when she read about it in the local newspaper. The few words mostly had four letters in them.

Apparently the pain Dad experienced was next level. Even now, he had a little gizmo where he could administer pain relief to himself when it got too bad. He kept his hand on it most times.

We talked about England. I told him everything Mum had said, the way she'd simply *stated* that I was going with her when Dad and I were better. Dad kinda smiled at that and pointed out it wasn't the greatest incentive for recovery. I also told him what Sam had said.

'I know that, Cate,' said Dad. 'I hit Mr Google hard the night we had dinner at your place. But thank Sam for me, will you?'

'Dad, you don't have to be nice all the time, you know,' I said. 'As far as me going to England is concerned, I get the feeling "nice" is not going to be part of Mum's vocabulary.'

'I will try to be horrible,' said Dad. 'But, look, Cate. We do need to talk about this. From my point of view, the thought of losing you is . . .' He screwed up his brow as if he knew the right word was there in his head somewhere, but he couldn't quite locate it. 'Unbearable,' he finished. 'But then I tell myself I can't lose you. Even if you're in England and I'm here in Australia, I won't have *lost* you.'

'More *misplaced* me?' I suggested.

Dad snorted and thumbed his pain gizmo. 'Don't make me laugh, you revolting child. You know what I mean.'

I did, though I still thought he was being too nice.

'In a few years,' Dad continued, 'you will be an adult and can make all your own choices. Maybe you'll come back to Australia. Maybe your home will be in Europe, or South America, who knows? Parents "lose" their kids that way all the time. In fact, loss is part of the job description. It's inevitable. I shouldn't complain. You're alive, no thanks to me, and that is more blessing than I can express.'

'Dad . . .'

'Cate, what do *you* want? Forget Mum. Forget me. Just for a moment, forget about all the . . . forces working on you right now. What do you want?'

It's what Elise had said, but it was so hard to do that. I'd spent my entire life thinking about my decisions in the context of other people – parents, teachers, even strangers in the street – and it was difficult to pin down what Caitlyn Carson wanted or needed. I wasn't really myself. I was also what other people *wanted* me to be.

'I want to stay here, Dad,' I said. 'I don't want to go to England. At least, not yet.'

Dad looked at me. But I felt . . . oh, it's difficult to express – relieved, maybe? No, not that. Just a certainty that what I'd said was what I wanted. I hadn't thought about it. I hadn't weighed advantages and disadvantages. This wasn't my brain speaking. It was something else. My heart. My gut. But in speaking those words a weight I hadn't known I was carrying lifted. I felt . . . light.

Maybe Dad saw that in my eyes.

'Are you sure that's what you want, Cate?'

'Yes. Certain.' I took his hand in mine. 'Mum will take this to court. I know that. She loves Sam and she has to be with him. She loves me and has to live with me. But sometimes it's not just about what *you* want, it's about what others need.'

'Did I say you'll be an adult in a few years?' said Dad. 'You're thirteen and more grown up than me.'

'Tell her you won't agree, Dad. Please. Tell her we'll both see her in court.'

Dad shifted awkwardly in his chair. I thought about offering to plump up his pillows, but I knew from experience that interference sometimes created pain, rather than soothing it.

'She'll win, you know,' said Dad. 'Even now, courts find it hard to give custody to fathers, even when they've been totally responsible. And after that accident no one could think of me as responsible. She will win and I suspect you know that.'

'Maybe.'

Dad raised an eyebrow.

'Probably,' I said. 'But that doesn't change what I want to do with my life. I think that's worth fighting for.'

Dad gazed at me a while longer and then nodded. 'Then we will fight.'

I smiled.

Dad held up a hand. 'As long as you understand that you can change your mind at any time and there will be no hard feelings. Okay?'

'Do you want to shake on it?' I asked.

'No,' said Dad. 'I want you to go. There are things going on with my bladder that a daughter should not get involved with. A nurse is on her way, so scoot.'

I scooted. But I felt good as I did it.

Sam's flight was at some ungodly hour, late on a Friday night. Mum had asked if I wanted to come to the airport and I'd agreed. I hadn't said anything to Sam about my decision and I certainly hadn't said anything to Mum. That was a conversation to have when there was just the two of us.

Even after check-in there were still two and a half hours until his plane took off, so we went to a cafe for a last drink. It was awkward. I thought there were probably things that Mum wanted to say to Sam and doubtless things he wanted to say to her. Mushy stuff that would offend my ears. Maybe I shouldn't have come, but then again, Mum probably wouldn't have come either if it meant leaving me home alone. So, after a fairly painful silence, I excused myself on the grounds I wanted to check out the bookshop opposite the cafe and left them to it.

I had to leave them to it again when Sam went through the gates that only passengers could go through. I gave him a quick hug, told him to WhatsApp me all the sights of London when he got there. He promised he would. So I beat a hasty retreat, though I watched from a distance as he and Mum hugged and kissed. It nearly brought tears to my eyes, but like I said, I'd given up tears on the grounds I'd shed way too many recently. But it was obvious that Mum could barely bring herself to let him go. When she finally did, she joined me with a fixed face and without a backward glance.

At least the trip home didn't take too long because, for once, the traffic out of Tullamarine wasn't disgusting.

Mostly we drove in silence. Mum was clearly emotional and I didn't think this was a good time to start our heart-to-heart. Plus it was nearly one thirty in the morning and I was tired. In fact, I think I dozed for a few minutes because when Mum spoke I jolted upright in the passenger seat.

'Sorry, what?' I said.

'I asked if you'd talked to your father yet.'

I could have said no. I probably should've said no.

'I won't come to England with you, Mum,' I said. 'And I will fight you in court, if I have to.'

Mum just nodded, as if she'd been expecting that, though the set of her jaw spoke louder and clearer than words.

We travelled the rest of the way without speaking. Even though I was exhausted, it still took me an hour or so of twisting and turning in my bed to drop off to sleep.

Dad stayed in hospital for a couple more weeks. Apparently, he could have been discharged earlier if he'd had someone to look after him at home. There was no one and I didn't want to ask about the woman in the restaurant. It also occurred to me to ask Mum if he could've stayed with us, but I didn't. I think maybe she would've said yes, but was it fair to ask her and Dad to stay in the same house when they were going to be fighting each other in court, presumably trashing each other's character in the process?

I tried to visit the hospital every day, but that wasn't possible. Sometimes Mum would take me and wait in the waiting room. Other times I'd get the train and the 59 tram. When Dad did finally get discharged, I knew that my weekend visitations were over. For one thing, Dad wouldn't be able to look after me. Not that I needed looking after, but thirteen-year-olds are supposed to have competent parental supervision. And that was the second reason. Mum wouldn't let me because Dad's supervision, in her opinion, was far from competent. Or maybe it was spite. Or revenge. So I went for short visits to his home – an hour here, a few hours there. He couldn't drive yet, so it was more train rides when Mum couldn't drive me or pick me up.

The first time I went to his house, he wanted to talk about the accident. It was a conversation that I guess had to happen sometime.

'I don't know how you can ever forgive me, Cate,' he said. 'I made you ride in a car without a seatbelt. I could've killed you. I nearly did.'

'I made a choice too, Dad,' I replied. 'I could've said no.'

He got agitated then – so agitated that I could see the little energy he still had evaporate.

'That's not the point. You're a child; you were in my care and I failed you.'

I sighed. Perhaps we did need to get this out in the open, if only so we could move on.

'Yeah. Okay. It was stupid, Dad. Stupid for you to suggest it, stupid of me to agree. But we were caught up in the story. In the story it made sense. Perhaps we should go a little easy on ourselves.'

'No. Doesn't work.' I wanted to calm him down. He was so tired and in so much pain, physical as well as emotional. But nothing was going to stop him. 'Bottom line here, Cate. I had to keep you safe. Not in a story. In the real world. I didn't. I know your mother will never forgive me. And she's right because I'll never forgive myself.'

'All right,' I said. 'You win. I'll never forgive you either. Now can we talk about something else?'

It worked. But only because I think he'd used up all his energy.

Most times I went to visit, Dad was so tired we'd often just sit and watch the television, though I would also make sure he had done his exercises. Once or twice I forced him to walk the two hundred metres to his local shop, so we could pick up stuff like toilet paper and microwave meals. I tried cooking for him. I looked up a simple menu for chilli con carne on my phone and I swear I followed the instructions to the letter. True, I boiled the rice to gloop and we couldn't eat that, but the chilli should've been fine. It wasn't. I've seen cat vomit that looked more appealing.

A couple of times Elise came with me and did some cooking. Don't get me wrong. El won't be a contestant on *MasterChef* anytime soon, but she can do basic stuff, like macaroni cheese. After my efforts, her mac cheese tasted like the food of the gods and she was happy to help us out. My decision to fight to stay in Australia had cheered her up no end. At least I *thought* it had.

One time, when I was at Dad's by myself, I saw an envelope on the small table next to his armchair and recognised Mum's handwriting. It was turned upside down and he had obviously opened it and read it, but he didn't say anything about what it contained. So I had to wait until he went to the toilet. It always took him an age, so I knew I'd have time to read it and put the letter back exactly the way I found it. Am I proud that I was going to read a private letter to Dad without his permission? Not really, but I didn't think I had a choice. I know my parents. Shit might be going on between the two of them, yet they would do all they could to keep me out of it. But this was my business as well as theirs. I felt I had a right.

*Dear Michael Carson,*

***Intention to permanently move to the United Kingdom with Caitlyn Rose Carson***

*As you are aware, it is my intention to emigrate from Australia to London, England, with our daughter, Caitlyn Rose Carson. It is my firm belief that this would be in the best interests of our daughter and provide her with opportunities that would broaden her mind and develop her potential. This letter is a formal request for your agreement in this proposal and would require written consent at your earliest*

*convenience. If this is not something you could immediately furnish and if you wish to discuss this matter further, we could make an appointment with an appropriate Compulsory Family Dispute Resolution practitioner as a way of avoiding court action, which would be distressing to all parties, especially Caitlyn.*
*I look forward to your response.*
*Yours sincerely,*
Lois Houseman

I put the letter back into the envelope and tried to make sure that it was in the same position I'd found it in. The toilet flushed a few minutes later and Dad hobbled back into his seat.

'Anything wrong, Cate?' he said as he sat. He must have done that thing where he was reading my face. How could I stop myself from writing on it?

'Nah,' I said. 'Indigestion, is all. Look, Dad, I have to go. Mum texted and said she'd be picking me up outside in a few minutes.'

'I'll see you out.'

'No need,' I said, and he looked grateful. Even a short walk to the toilet and back had exhausted him. I left him staring at the television, his brow slightly furrowed with pain. I closed the front door quietly.

I walked a few minutes to the local park, sat on a bench and watched as mums (and a few dads) looked over their kids on the playground swings and roundabouts.

I wondered how many of those mothers and fathers would go through what my parents were going through, when passion turned to indifference, when declarations of burning love turned to cold language in formal letters. It wasn't very chilly outside, but I shivered anyway.

I walked home. It took nearly two hours, but I didn't care.

Sam kept his word. He sent me messages and videos at least once a day. It was a WhatsApp group that contained just the two of us. I knew he had one with Mum where they could talk of stuff not suitable for my eyes and ears.

Most of the videos were of his trips to tourist sites. Buckingham Palace and the Changing of the Guard – those soldiers in their silly hats – Hyde Park, Big Ben and the Houses of Parliament, Westminster Abbey, London markets, big red buses driving down streets. Sam gave a running commentary and they were normally funny, complaining about the weather and the crushes on the Underground and the prices of . . . almost everything. They were great and I looked forward to receiving them, even when I suspected they were little more than propaganda. Mum must've known I was getting them, but she never asked. Maybe she was keeping quiet and hoping they would work their own type of magic.

The days passed. Most of the time I pretended to forget that beneath the deafening silence from my parents there was a war being waged. A war over me.

Then, on the day before I was due to go back to school, I got a phone call from Elise's mother. El was in hospital. She was fine, but she'd had her stomach pumped, because she'd swallowed as many of her mother's tablets as she could find in the medicine cabinet in her parents' ensuite bathroom.

# CHAPTER ELEVEN

★

'I'm sorry,' said Elise. She was propped up in her hospital bed and she looked pale and fragile and . . . empty. I don't know how else to describe it. Something had sucked the spirit out of my best friend.

'You have nothing to be sorry about,' I said. It wasn't the best response but I couldn't come up with anything else.

'It was a crazy thing to do,' she said, but she couldn't meet my eyes. 'A few tablets that wouldn't have hurt me if I'd taken another hundred. I couldn't even do that right. I just made myself look stupid.'

A number of replies crossed my mind.

*No, you didn't.*

*You're never stupid.*

*If you think you look stupid, what about me? My best friend needed me and I was nowhere to be found.*

I didn't say anything. There was nothing to say really.

So I just held her hand until the nurse told me I had to leave. Then I went to the waiting room, where her parents were sitting, heads bowed.

Here's what I wanted to say: *Your daughter is in more pain than you can understand, mainly because you refuse to see beyond your own.*

I didn't say that, because it applied equally to me. How had I not seen the signs? Oh, they'd been there, now I thought back. The eyes brimming with tears, the twisted smiles. But I'd only paid attention to the jokes. It's what El and I do. I knew how Dad felt. Sometimes you do or don't do things that either put people in danger or simply fail to protect them. I'd been blind to what was going on with Elise and I would never forgive myself.

I told her parents what I intended to do. They didn't argue, which was surprising in one way but not in another. I also told them that my father would take responsibility, if it all became too impractical as the divorce progressed. I hadn't asked Dad, but I knew he wouldn't let me down. And it would probably do him good, if push came to shove. Then I went home, hit the internet and struck gold almost immediately. I gave a sharp intake of breath at the price, but then again I hadn't really known what to do with my winnings from the Premier's award. They'd just sat there in my bank account, dozing quietly. Time to nudge them awake.

Of course, there was still Liam Cooper to deal with, but I didn't think that was going to be a big problem.

Money can't buy happiness, apparently, but maybe it can rent some for a time.

Neither Mum nor Dad were forthcoming when I asked what was going on with the court case and what stage we had reached. I brought the subject up over a particularly dismal dinner but Mum absolutely refused to discuss it. At first. I had to admit that maybe she had a point.

'In many ways, Cate,' she said, 'I am going to be up against *you* in court, rather than your father. My understanding is that he would probably not fight this, but that you are the driving force behind his opposition . . .'

I tried to interrupt, but she held up her hand.

'He hasn't said anything to me, by the way,' she continued. 'And my lawyer has advised me not to talk to either you or your father about this. Things . . . have a habit of turning nasty, apparently. I don't want that to happen and I'm pretty sure your dad doesn't either.' She brushed hair away from her forehead. Was it my imagination or were there more lines there recently? 'Please think carefully about all this, Cate. I think you will lose in court. I think you will be going to England with me. Do you really want all three of us to go through hell when it won't change the outcome? How is your father going to feel when he loses and you could've avoided all that pain?'

It was then I got angry. I mean, stand up, throw things, smash plates kind of angry.

'Thanks, Mum,' I said. 'I mean, huge thanks. I didn't ask for all this. I didn't ask for you guys to get divorced. I didn't ask for you to start seeing Sam and I sure as hell didn't ask that we move to England, taking me away from my father and my best friend . . . my best friend who needs me . . .' I was starting to choke on my words and that just made me angrier. 'And now *I'm* responsible? Is that it? I should just do whatever *you* think is good for me so I can spare people pain. Well, hello, Mum? Daughter in pain here and I will not feel guilty just because you don't want things to get nasty. Hate to tell you, but they're already nasty, Mum. My life is turning to shit and you don't care.'

I didn't smash anything, but I did go straight to my room. Mum left me to stew, which was good and probably wise. Stewing was exactly what I wanted.

The familiarity of my bedroom calmed me a little. When my heart stopped hammering, I *tried* to look at the whole thing logically. Did Mum have a point? Who was I to cause so much upset? I'd been critical of Elise's parents for putting their daughter through unnecessary pain, but wasn't I doing the same to everyone I cared about? Then I thought again. Good old logical Cate. Caring about everyone, being nice, protecting the feelings of other people and not paying attention to mine or Elise's. I was done with it. Done with being walked over.

I tried to do some writing, where I had control over one world at least, the one in my head. But then I saw it as another stupid way of avoiding reality. It was just a game, a story like Dad and I would create, and it wouldn't lead anywhere. I was done with that, too.

I had difficulty sleeping that night and when I did, I had restless and troubled dreams involving suffocating loss.

Dad tried to take the same approach as Mum, keeping me in the dark, which got me angry again. I pointed out that *I* was the one who wanted to fight and it therefore didn't make any sense to pretend I wasn't there. Eventually, Dad agreed. He said his lawyer had asked to meet me anyway.

'You've got a lawyer, Dad?' I said.

'Of course,' he replied. 'Who did you think I'd be employing, Cate? A plumber? Mind you, there probably wouldn't be much difference in cost. They both charge like a wounded bull.'

'How much?' This was something I hadn't thought about. Maybe I should've put my own savings into the pot. But there was only a hundred or so left, after I'd seen Liam Cooper, and that wasn't going to get us very far.

'Enough,' said Dad.

'Can you afford it?'

'I've already paid. Well, a large whack of it. There'll be a final bill, I dare say.'

'If we pull out, will you get a refund?'

Dad laughed.

'You're only thirteen, Cate, so I shouldn't be surprised

that you don't know how lawyers work. No. I won't get a refund. Why? Are you having second thoughts?'

'No. Of course not.' That wasn't strictly true (the old reasonable Cate kept trying to make an appearance and sometimes – most times, to be honest – I listened to her), but I couldn't tell Dad he'd wasted whatever money he'd already spent. Then again, shouldn't I protect him from spending even more money on something we probably wouldn't win?

I wished I hated my parents. I wished I was sixteen, could leave home and live with a boyfriend they'd both hate. Someone with tattoos and no source of income.

I had difficulty sleeping that night and when I did, I had restless and troubled dreams involving suffocating feelings of emotional and financial loss.

Mr Lee was very nice and friendly. He wheeled himself from behind his desk and shook me by the hand. Right from the start he didn't treat me like I was some kind of naive kid, even though I felt like a naive kid.

'It is a pleasure to meet you, Caitlyn,' he said. 'Your father has told me a lot about you.'

'Mostly lies, I expect,' I said.

He laughed dutifully.

'Can I get you a drink?' he asked.

'I'm fine,' said Dad.

'I would like a glass of water, please,' I said. I thought I might as well get something other than legal advice for

Dad's money. Assuming the water was free, of course. Mr Lee pressed something on his desk phone and asked for water to be brought in. Then he inched his wheelchair a little closer and looked straight into my eyes.

'I believe you would like to know the state of play, Caitlyn,' he said.

I nodded.

'At present,' he said, 'we are in the stage where we are trying to avoid court.'

'I thought that was impossible,' I said. Then I felt bad for interrupting.

'It probably is,' he said. 'Unless your mother changes her mind about going to England or you and your father change your minds about fighting it. From everything I understand, both of these outcomes are unlikely.'

I nodded again.

'But there are still good reasons why we have to go through certain processes before going straight into a courtroom. The judge in the Federal Circuit Court who hears your case will want to be assured that all parties have tried to settle their disputes before enforcing a legal judgement. Do you understand?'

'Yes.'

'Good. This means that in the next week or so you will be visited by a mediator from a Family Dispute Resolution organisation. This will almost certainly be Anglicare, who have a contract with the family court. They have considerable experience in these matters. By the way, Caitlyn, jump in with questions whenever you like.'

There was a pause while a young man brought in a jug of water and three glasses. I poured myself a glass as he closed the door softly behind him.

'Mum isn't going to change her mind,' I said. 'And neither will we. So isn't that just a waste of time?'

Mr Lee smiled.

'If you were to refuse mediation on the grounds it was a waste of time, then almost certainly your father would be liable for the legal costs incurred by your mother. I imagine that would be something you'd want to avoid.'

I was beginning to realise just how little I knew about the consequences of what I had set in motion.

'The court will also want to know about your living arrangements with both parties – the kind of care each can provide – as well as their respective financial situations. Remember, Caitlyn, it is your interest and your interest only that the court will be concerned about. Who can look after you best, both financially and emotionally.'

I glanced at Dad. He was examining his fingernails and seemed calm. These were factors he was obviously familiar with.

'Will our car accident be brought up in court?' I asked.

'Absolutely,' said Mr Lee. 'And your mother's lawyer will argue that this is one reason why your father shouldn't have permanent custody, that he cannot be trusted with your welfare.'

'What arguments would we give?'

'That one mistake shouldn't condemn a parent absolutely. Everyone makes mistakes.'

I sipped my water. I was beginning to think things through for the first time. Before, it had seemed like some kind of game – a simple game where there was going to be a winner and a loser and where my wishes would be paramount. I hadn't fully realised that this was a fight where the rules were totally outside my experience.

'Tell me what my mother's lawyer will say,' I asked.

Mr Lee poured himself a glass of water and took a sip. He interlocked his fingers and gazed at a point just above my head.

'She will say that at thirteen years of age you need a mother to navigate all the problems associated with puberty and adolescence. She will point out that your father doesn't have a woman in his life, whereas your mother has a partner, Sam Ellis, who can provide you with a father figure. She will say that Mr Ellis has an excellent, well-paying job and that your mother stands a very good chance of finding employment as a teacher in the UK. Your father, on the other hand, isn't financially ... stable. Although he may well have insurance from the car accident, given it wasn't his fault, and this might cover loss of earnings while he recovers, he will still struggle to provide for himself, let alone you. She will argue that the games you play when you stay over with him are evidence of a psychological problem, that he is adolescent in his attitude. She may well suggest that your mother pays for psychiatric experts to give opinions on your father's suitability as a lone parent and that these opinions be entered into evidence.'

There was a long silence. It felt like someone had punched me in the stomach.

'Thanks for your honesty,' I said.

'You wanted to know,' he said. 'And your father, and I, for what it's worth, think you're entitled to know.'

'Is it completely hopeless?'

'Not at all.' Mr Lee unlocked his fingers and leaned forward. Once again, he looked me straight in the eyes. 'If staying in Australia with your father is what you want then we will fight for that. Court cases are not foregone conclusions. Your father is a good parent and we can prove that.'

'Can I give evidence?'

'I think that would be an excellent idea. I suggest you prepare a statement to be read out in court, assuming we get that far. But you should understand that this will mean you can be cross-examined by your mother's lawyer.'

He must have seen a hint of panic in my eyes.

'It's not like the TV,' he said. 'No lawyer is going to think it's a good idea to rip into a thirteen-year-old in court. But she will almost certainly ask you questions.' He glanced at his watch. 'Now, I do have an appointment in five minutes. But is there anything you'd like to ask?'

I knew that as soon as we were outside, all kinds of questions would occur to me. But right now, I couldn't think of anything. Next time, I thought, I'd be better prepared. I'd come with a whole list of questions.

Dad and I walked down the street to a bus stop, both lost in our own thoughts. While we sat on a bench and waited I told him about Elise and what I intended to do. He whistled when I told him the part involving him.

'You didn't think it was a good idea to talk this over with me first, Cate?'

'I thought you might say no.'

'You thought right.'

'And that's why it wasn't a good idea to talk it over with you. Come on, Dad. It almost certainly won't happen and even if it does, it will help with your physiotherapy.'

Dad laughed. That was a good sign. We needed laughter and it had been in short supply recently.

Elise and I sat at our normal bench at lunch and watched schoolkids as they went past. She'd only been off school for a week and I was surprised to see her back so soon, but she'd told me that staying at home was not an option.

'Don't get me wrong, CC,' she said. 'They haven't argued, even when I was in my room. They're trying hard and not just when I'm around. I think.'

'Any chance they might stay together?'

Elise tucked one leg up under her and played with her hair. I'd always wished I could tuck a leg under my bum the way she can but when I tried I got the worst case of cramps ever. She's just flexible, is El.

'Nah,' she said. 'Not going to happen and it would be shit if it did. They'd only be together for me and that's no reason. No. All I'm hoping is they stay civilised until it's all over.'

'Civilised is good,' I said.

'I did some checking on the internet about divorces gone bad,' said El. 'You wouldn't believe some of the shit parents pull. The lies that are told, including bogus accusations of sexual abuse against their own children.'

'You're kidding.'

'I wish. Seems that sometimes love can turn to a kind of crazy hate. You've read about this, CC. People who kill their own kids just to stop the other person having them.'

I knew she was right. But those were people whose stories were in newspapers or on television reports. They didn't live next door to you. You didn't *know* them. And therefore they weren't really real, they were just characters in a drama. Then I remembered that someone once said psychopaths had to live next door to *someone*. A shiver ran down my spine.

I asked how she was doing. Well, I didn't use those words. In fact, I skirted around the subject in what I hoped was a discreet enquiry into her mental health. But one of the good things about being best friends is that you can see straight through that stuff. I suppose it's one of the bad things as well.

'I'm not going to try it again, CC,' she said. 'If that's what you're asking.'

'No, I wasn't asking that.' I stopped myself and thought for a moment. 'Actually, that's exactly what I'm asking. So you're good?'

'"Good" might be too strong a word,' she replied. 'But I'll survive.'

'Survival is definitely good,' I said.

Then she asked how my custody battle was going and I filled her in on the meeting with Dad's lawyer. El frowned when I told her what Mum's lawyer was going to be saying about Dad.

'Here's hoping both sets of 'rents stay civilised,' she said.

'Civilised is definitely good,' I replied.

'Excuse me?'

El and I glanced up.

Liam Cooper stood next to our bench. He looked very nervous and he was switching weight between one foot and another. His face was flushed.

'Elise Carmichael,' he said. 'You should know that I am not fit to kiss the dirt beneath your feet.'

# CHAPTER TWELVE

★

There was a stunned silence that seemed to last for most of the lunch break. Liam swayed from foot to foot and then reached into his pocket and took out a piece of paper. He glanced at me as if for permission and I nodded. He unfolded the paper and cleared his throat.

'Elise,' he said. 'You are the very peak of perfection and I am less than the dust beneath your chariot wheels. It is obvious that someone of your stunning natural beauty and impe . . . impecc . . .'

'Impeccable,' I said.

'Impeccable personality will have suitors falling over themselves to vee for your favours.'

'That's "vie", Liam,' I chipped in.

'Whatever,' he said. 'I understand that I have no chance of being your favoured partner on the grounds I am a jock with the . . .'

He looked at me again and I nodded for him to carry

on. Liam swallowed and held the paper up.

'. . . the mental ability of a lower private . . .'

'Primate,' I said.

'Whatever. And I will therefore not embarrass myself by courting you anymore, since rejection is inevitable. I may be . . .'

He looked at me again and if looks could kill, I'd be curling my toes at that very moment. But I wasn't going to let him off. I made my gaze steely and nodded towards his paper.

'I may be uglier than a bucketful of bumholes,' he continued, 'but I have a parting gift that is as beautiful as I am revolting.' He reached into his pocket again and pulled out an envelope, handed it to Elise. 'It is at your friend's house, but here is a picture for you to enjoy for the time being.'

I pulled out an envelope from my pocket and handed it over to Liam. He snatched it and hissed at me. 'Better be all here and if anyone hears about this . . .'

I held up a hand.

'You have my word, Liam. Just between the three of us.'

I would have preferred it if he'd left us before opening my envelope but I guess he'd used up all his restraint by then. He fanned the four fifty-dollar bills and held them up to the light like he was checking to see if they were forgeries. I didn't have much confidence that Liam Cooper would be able to spot a forgery if it bit him in the leg, but I guess he was entitled to be a bit snarky. Then he turned on his heel and stormed off.

I looked at Elise. Elise looked at me.

Then she had a fit of laughing that I thought would never stop. She clutched at her stomach, she bent herself double, she screamed as tears ran down her face. It was the kind of laughter you can't help but share. We both laughed until it hurt. After what seemed like an hour we wheezed into silence.

'You cannot mention this to anyone, Elise,' I said. 'If you do, Liam will apparently find out and there will be recriminations involving the spilling of blood. All of it mine, according to Mr Cooper.'

She made the zipping movement with her hand across her mouth.

'You paid him two hundred bucks to give that speech, CC? You crazy?'

'Yes, but that's not the issue right now. Aren't you going to open that envelope?'

She turned it over in her hands.

'Why would you give Liam Cooper two hundred bucks to read out a speech? Don't get me wrong, CC. Hilarious and everything, but that's gotta be the world's most expensive joke. Makes no sense.'

'He wanted three hundred. I had to bargain him down,' I said. 'Even then, there were conditions. No one could see him and no one could hear of it ever again. He was most firm on that last point.'

'Still makes no sense.'

I sighed and glanced at my phone. The bell ending lunch recess would be going in about five minutes.

'If I explain, El, will you open that envelope?'

She just tilted her head.

'Okay, here's a shortened version,' I said. 'You remember when I told you that two men sang me a song at St Kilda beach?'

'That beautiful but shit song. Yeah.'

'Dad arranged that. He makes dramas we can share. He writes scripts and we play them out. But we don't let the other know that we know. It's a game.'

She wrinkled her brow in confusion.

'So what, this was a game? You paid Liam Cooper two hundred bucks for a comedy routine?'

'Kind of,' I said. 'Think of it as more of a show. But that's not the important part.' I nodded towards the envelope she was still turning over and over. 'The main thing is in there.' I wasn't going to tell her that two hundred bucks was small potatoes compared to what I'd spent on the main thing. 'Think of Liam as the starter.' I touched the envelope with my index finger. 'That's the main course.'

She opened it then. Elise slid the photograph out and looked at it. For a few seconds she didn't seem to understand. Then a single tear appeared at the corner of her right eye. It swelled and ran down her cheek.

'A Saint Bernard puppy,' I said, just in case her brain had shut down completely. 'Ten weeks old, fully vaccinated and complete with pedigree certificate.'

'But . . .'

'Your parents know. You will be able to keep it at

home. If something happens – if it all turns bad in some way – my father will take it in. You can visit, take it for walks. But it will still be your dog.'

I took her by the hand.

'But it won't come to that, El,' I added. 'Your parents know they owe you something for all the pain you've been through. And are still going through. They hope this goes a small way to paying off that debt.'

'They bought this puppy?'

'Ah, well. No. I did. But trust me, they *will* be paying. Do you have any idea how much it costs to keep a Saint Bernard in dog food? I mean, they grow to be the size of a horse. Apparently, you don't need a dog bowl and a scoop for the biscuits. You need a wheelbarrow and a shovel.'

The tears continued to run down Elise's face.

'This isn't a joke, is it, CC? Because if it is, I'll never forgive you.'

'No joke. The puppy is in our laundry room at home. Mum took me to pick it up last night. She was firm about a couple of points. If she craps or wees, then I have to clean it up. The pup, that is. Not Mum. Secondly, it has to be gone by tonight. That, I believe, is where you come in, El.'

Elise stood and cleaned away the remains of our food just as the bell signalling the end of lunch rang.

'Two more lessons, El,' I said, 'and you'll be meeting your new best friend.'

'The hell with that,' said El. 'We're going now.'

'You want to wag school? We can't do that.'

'Watch me, CC.'

And I thought. I'd nearly died. Elise had tried to harm herself. Her parents were ripping each other's throats out. My mother wanted to tear me away from my father and my friends. A court case loomed. Horrible things were going to be said. I was probably going to be relocated from the only country I'd ever known to an unfamiliar place just so that Mum could continue loving someone who was still, in some ways, a stranger to me.

And I was worried about missing a couple of lessons? I grabbed my backpack.

'You're gonna love her, El,' I promised.

'I love her already.'

'Not more than me, though.'

'Course not.' Elise stopped and put a finger on her chin. 'Who the freaking hell are you again?'

We linked arms and strode through the school gates as if we didn't have a care in the world. A teacher shouted something at us, but we didn't even look back.

The dog *had* peed. And crapped. It was difficult to believe something so small could have produced so much waste. And it stank. I nearly gagged when we opened the laundry door. El just fell to her knees and swept the pup up in her arms. She started doing the hysterical crying thing again. I mean, I know they were tears of happiness, but even so . . .

'I'll clear up the mess, CC,' she said through her tears.

'If you insist,' I replied. Luckily there were mops and buckets already in the laundry room, though one of the mops had been shredded by something with small but sharp teeth. There was a prime suspect I had in mind, but I kept my thoughts to myself. El couldn't bring herself to let the dog go while she cleaned, which made for a somewhat bizarre and funny spectacle. She didn't do a bad job and it probably helped that the poo was more liquid than solid (I'd put bleach down the laundry sink later), but she failed to realise that the hem of her school skirt had a suspicious stain from when she'd fallen to her knees amid a sea of urine. I thought it best not to point it out.

'We'll walk her home, CC,' said El. There was a kind of wild glint in her eyes. 'It'll only take an hour or so.'

'Ah,' I said. 'Though tiny beastie here does have a collar and a lead, she won't be able to go walking through the streets for a few more weeks yet. She needs her parvo booster. Mum said she'd drive us later when she gets back from work.'

El had difficulty hiding her disappointment.

'But our backyard,' I added, 'will be a wilderness for her to explore. I bought toys, Elise.'

And the next couple of hours were glorious. I don't know about Elise, but for that time I forgot all about the problems we were tangled up in. We threw toys for the tiny Saint Bernard and she chased them or didn't or went after her own tail or sniffed at things in the garden beds.

She played with all the abandon of something crazily young. We did too.

'We wagged school this arvo, Mum,' I said. I figured she would probably find out in time. In my experience parents *always* find out stuff you don't want them to know. Every single freaking time. There's probably a law of physics about it.

'My fault,' said El. She had the dog in a bear hug that was so tight it was vaguely worrying. The pup didn't appear fussed though.

'But Cate's responsibility,' said Mum.

'I figured it wasn't going to make much difference,' I said. 'You know, given I'll miss school for weeks if we go to England. Not to mention being put into a system I know nothing about. What's a couple of lessons compared to all that?'

Mum gave me a look. If I had to be specific, I would call it a *Mum* look. All kids know it. It's the one that says, *you and I will be having words later, Miss Smart-Arse.* But she kept quiet for now.

On our way over to her place later, Elise sat in the back seat and crooned to the dog in her lap. The front was occupied by tension. From time to time, Mum's nose crinkled as if she'd caught a whiff of dog urine clinging to a school uniform, but I might have been mistaken. Mum walked El to the front door, and smiled and chatted to El's mum for a minute or two while I waited in the car.

I waved as my friend went inside. I couldn't remember when I'd seen her so happy.

The journey back was uneventful for at least a minute.

'Your father and I were in court today,' said Mum.

# CHAPTER THIRTEEN

★

'Tennis or badminton?' I asked. I didn't want to make a joke, but I didn't know what else to say.

'It's called a duty list,' said Mum. 'Where we file all the documents relating to the case. You know, the findings from the Family Dispute Resolution officer and other things.'

It was difficult to forget the visit to the FDR mediator. Mum and Dad agreed that I should be present at the meeting on the grounds that I was mature enough to deal with the issues, and that my wishes were, after all, the main reason we were in this situation in the first place. The mediator – a very friendly woman who insisted we call her Helen – suggested that we all meet at her office rather than coming to our home, because that would be 'neutral territory'. The meeting took about two hours and was civilised enough. Helen encouraged all of us to discuss the issues fully, to pinpoint exactly what the problems were and how they could be resolved. But I think it was fairly obvious to everyone that this was not something like agreeing to financial settlements or access arrangements. Mum wanted me to go to England. I didn't. Dad supported me. It wasn't a situation where compromise could figure, unless we all moved to somewhere in between, like Myanmar.

In the end the mediator issued something called a Section 601 Certificate, which basically called for the case to be heard in the Family Circuit Court by a judge. A week or so after that, some woman turned up at Mum's home on a Saturday morning and watched as Mum and I did our normal mother and daughter stuff, like me resisting doing dishes or vacuuming the front room but always giving in eventually. The woman poked her head into my bedroom (after asking my permission) and talked to me and Mum in general terms. Then she left. 'Who the hell was that?' I asked Mum. 'Someone checking that I am not a psychopath,' Mum replied. 'She'll be visiting your father as well.' I didn't give it much more thought. Well, I did, but it didn't help very much.

I shook my head to get rid of the memories.

'You didn't tell me you were going to court,' I said.

Mum checked her rear-view mirror, merged into traffic.

'No point,' she said. 'It was all routine. Just the four of us – your father and his lawyer and me with mine. The judge understood that nothing could be resolved in an interim hearing and she fixed a date for the final hearing, when a decision will be made.'

My mouth was dry. Things were happening too quickly. At the back of my mind I must have been hoping that something would change, though I couldn't think what that might be. Now there was a date.

'When?' I asked.

'Monday. Two weeks today,' said Mum. 'You will have to take the day off school. Maybe a few days, if the case drags on. Though I suppose taking time away from school won't bother you too much.'

She glanced at me and smiled to show she wasn't being shitty, but I couldn't respond because the muscles in my face weren't obeying me.

Two weeks. My future, or at the very least a large part of it, would be determined in two weeks by a total stranger. I was scared.

'What are you going to call her?'

Elise's backyard wasn't huge, but that didn't seem to matter to her or the pup. El rolled on her back while the dog jumped on her, pretend-growling and having small nibbles at her feet and hands.

'Ow,' said Elise. 'Ya mongrel.'

'Not a mongrel, El,' I pointed out. 'Definitely not a mongrel.'

'True,' said El. 'Ow, ya pedigree.' She played with the Saint Bernard's ears. 'I don't know,' she continued. 'If you're buggering off, I might call her CC. You know, give me a reason to say your name.'

This was almost unbearably sad, because she wasn't joking for once. I told her about the court date. We sat on her lawn in silence for a few minutes while the pup explored smells along a fence line.

'So how long before the judge makes a decision?' she said finally. 'Like, could be months later, yeah?'

'I googled that,' I said. 'Possibly the same day.'

'Shit.'

'The case might take a few days,' I continued, 'but Mum reckons it won't because no one is bringing crap loads of witnesses or anything. Should just be arguments by both lawyers, my statement, a cross examination. It all depends. One day, possibly two. And the judge *might* delay judgement.' I gave the pup a liver treat from my pocket. She wagged her tail and El and I fell a little bit more in love. 'But both Mum and Dad reckon that's unlikely as well. It's a pretty straightforward decision and Mum will be arguing that there's some urgency.'

'And if the judge is on your mum's side, when would you go?'

I shrugged. 'Mum says quickly after that. A few weeks, probably. Her granddad was a UK citizen, she says, so she can apply for an Ancestry visa which allows her to work and live in England for up to five years. But I suspect she'll be marrying Sam, anyway. And Sam has dual citizenship. Permanent residence in England is not going to be a problem, especially since we're all vaxxed to the eyeballs.'

'What do you reckon are your chances, CC?'

'Not good.' I sighed. 'Dad's lawyer says it's not a foregone conclusion, that the days when mothers automatically get custody are long gone. But Dad is paying him. It's unlikely he'd say we have no chance when he's being paid to make sure that no chance isn't an option. But I can read Dad's eyes. Oh, he's upbeat, but he doesn't think he's going to win.'

'So we might only have four weeks left,' said Elise.

'Better make the most of them then,' I replied.

Two days before the court case, I got a phone call from a number I didn't recognise. I'd been getting a few of those recently – some of them came with warnings of suspected fraud and some played recorded messages informing me that there was a warrant out for my arrest for non-payment of non-existent tax bills. To be honest, there aren't too many people outside my immediate family and Elise who have my number. So I wasn't very optimistic when I answered the call.

'Hello?' I said.

'I'm trying to reach Caitlyn Carson,' said a woman's voice at the other end of the line. The voice sounded somewhat puzzled, as if I was obviously *not* Caitlyn Carson and was trying to confuse her for reasons best known to myself.

'That's me,' I replied.

'Oh . . .' There was quite a long pause. When she spoke again, it was with a tone of greater confidence. 'My name is Mo Axon and I'm a commissioning publisher at Blake McDonald Publishing House. I'm ringing in relation to the manuscript of *Unicorn Girl*, which was passed onto me by Jane Brown of the Book Pitch Program. That *is* your manuscript, right?'

I hadn't forgotten about the book. Of course I hadn't. But it had somehow slipped down my list of priorities after everything that had been happening. Now my heart threatened to break out through my ribs. I mean, I know I had given up writing, but . . .

'Yes,' I said. 'That's me. I wrote that. *Unicorn Girl*. That's mine.' I couldn't remember the last time I had been so much in control of words. Mo Axon couldn't fail to be impressed.

'Ah. Look. I should say immediately that I don't think we will be publishing your book . . .'

There was a ringing in my ears and I missed the rest of what she was saying. Yes. Okay. What on earth was I expecting? Come on, Cate. I knew that the chances of getting published were really slim. Hell, JK Rowling was rejected twelve times for *Harry Potter*, so what chance did I realistically have? For all that, I hadn't realised how much I had been hoping for a miracle until I heard those words of rejection. They hit me in the gut. I wanted to cry, but I wasn't going to allow that to happen. I'd made some kind of pledge to myself. Caitlyn Carson was not going to cry anymore. Not for anything short of death.

So why was Mo Axon ringing me now? Was everyone in the office of Blake McDonald bored and listening around the phone as she rang? Was Mo Axon going to say, *We think your book's crap!* before hanging up? I wished it had been someone telling me there was a warrant out for my arrest unless I paid my non-existent tax bill with iTunes gift cards. I could've laughed at that.

'Hello?' The voice at the other end was still there.

'I'm sorry,' I said. 'I didn't hear that last bit after you said you weren't going to publish *Unicorn Girl*. I think the line dropped out.'

'I asked how old you are.'

I nearly answered automatically, but caught myself in time.

'Does my age matter?' I asked. Then I wondered if I came across as someone who was getting pissy because they'd been rejected and wished I'd just answered. This phone call was a nightmare from the start and getting worse by the moment.

'No,' said Mo Axon. 'Not to the book and not to our decision to publish. But I'm curious. You sound very young.'

'I'm thirteen,' I said.

There was a long pause.

'You're joking,' she said finally.

I thought about replying, *What part of 'I'm thirteen' has you in hysterics?* But I thought it wiser to say nothing.

'Caitlyn,' she continued. 'Please listen carefully. I know you must be disappointed, but you should understand that I do not normally ring up writers we are rejecting. In the vast majority of cases that is done by our commissioning editor. Even then, it's normally by email.'

'Okay,' I said.

'I think your writing has enormous potential and I wanted to discuss things with you in person. Because I really believe we will be publishing you in the future.'

'Okay,' I said again.

'I was going to suggest that we meet up for a meal in Melbourne to discuss your writing, but given you're thirteen I suppose that's not going to work.'

'Okay.'

'How would it be if I came to your house and talked everything over with you and your parents?'

'Okay,' I said. I knew there were other words available to me, but they seemed to have left my brain for destinations unknown.

We talked for another few minutes. I gave her my address. We arranged a time, about four or five days after my court case.

I don't know why I bothered. Probably because the old polite Cate had moved back in to stay. But the publisher didn't think my book was worth publishing. There was no way round that.

Giving up writing was a good decision, whichever way you looked at it. But now I'd have to put up with someone telling me that failure was something positive. I could do without it.

# CHAPTER FOURTEEN

★

The Sunday before my court case I was allowed to stay at Elise's for the night. I think this was partly so Mum and I could avoid all those tense silences when we avoided discussing the case. Or maybe avoid all those tense conversations where the subject of the case was avoided.

Avoidance figured largely in my household.

Dad and his lawyer were going to pick me up in the morning and then head straight to court. Elise was going to go to school. She wanted to come to the court to support me, but I was told that children weren't allowed, unless it was by special dispensation from the judge. That took time and there wasn't enough. I *really* could've done with Elise there and no one had told me it wasn't possible. There it was again: no part of my life was under my control.

The puppy had got her parvo booster and the vet told Elise she was allowed out for walks. It was kinda hilarious, though, because the pup had no idea how to behave on a leash. Or off a leash, to be honest. She got an idea in her head and she went for it. Chasing a bike? Good idea. Barking at a tree? Why not? Turning round, sniffing, going in circles, wrapping her lead around lampposts, getting the leash caught up around Elise's ankles, taking a dump in the middle of the footpath? All part of life's rich tapestry, it would seem. And judging by the grin on her little face, everything life offered was just . . . magnificent. There were lessons to be learned here, but I couldn't just enjoy the moment as she seemed to. The future and all its dark possibilities stood in my way.

Elise was in love, though. She was amazingly patient. She cleaned up poo without apparently giving it a second thought. When she tickled the pup's tummy and it gave her a play bite that drew blood, she didn't flinch. This was a marriage that was never going to be threatened.

Speaking of which, her parents were very friendly and there wasn't even a hint of conflict. When they looked at the puppy it was with something approaching horror, though they tried to hide it. But they didn't say anything and even gave it the occasional pat. It wasn't allowed in the kitchen when anyone was cooking, though.

'She drools like crazy,' Elise explained. 'And the internet reckons it'll get worse the older she gets. Put food anywhere near her and it's like turning a tap on. I'll show ya.'

She held out a piece of liver snack that she produced from her pocket and I have to confess I was impressed. I hadn't realised anything could produce drool totally out of proportion to its size. If we'd been in a boat I would've thought we'd sprung a leak. It was gross.

'Isn't that cute?' said Elise.

'You bet,' I said.

When it was time for bed, Elise took the dog to the laundry room. Apparently, this was a condition that her parents had insisted on and I couldn't really blame them. What with wee and poo and drool, this puppy had serious leakage issues at both ends. It wouldn't have been pretty if she'd been allowed to sleep in Elise's room. Then again, it was pitiful when we put her in there and closed the door. She immediately started whining. Elise *and* the pup, actually.

'Saint Bernards are the most loving and loyal dogs,' she said between sobs as we went up the stairs to her bedroom. 'She's bonded with me already. When we're apart she's like totally heartbroken. So am I.'

At least we couldn't hear the dog whining when we closed El's door, and I was grateful. I knew that tomorrow would be stressful and I'd need to get in as many zs as possible. Sure, Elise and I would chat for a few hours, but I'd be asleep by midnight if I could keep those random, troubling visions of the court out of my mind.

Elise has a king bed, which helps when you're trying to find space, especially since El has a habit of starfishing when she's asleep. I've been woken a number of times during sleepovers at her place by a random smack in the face at three in the morning. I curl up on the edge of the bed and that's generally safe. Generally.

'Now where's my baby monitor app?' said El.

'Excuse me?'

'It's gotta be here somewhere . . .'

I propped myself up on an elbow.

'El, I could've sworn you just talked about finding your "baby monitor app"'

'Yup. I've lost it. Ah, here it is . . .'

'Is there something you haven't told me about you and Liam Cooper?'

'What?' Elise fumbled with her phone. 'Wait a moment. Just opening it up.'

She held up her phone so we could both see the screen. The Saint Bernard puppy was turning in circles and didn't seem happy. Off to the side was a dark patch that was obviously poo. Not very solid poo either. As we watched, the dog squatted and did a wee.

'Stress because she's separated from me,' said Elise. 'You can't blame her.'

'Indeed,' I said. 'I do the same when you're not around.'

The dog had only been on her own for a few minutes. At this rate, she'd fill the laundry room in a couple of hours. At least she wasn't drooling. Yet.

'You watch her at night?' I said. Okay, it wasn't the quickest conclusion I'd ever come to, but my brain wasn't performing at its best.

'Course.' She fiddled with the side of the phone and the dog's howling filled the room. 'Got my phone paired with an iPad set up in the laundry room. I need to look after her.'

'Elise, please. Put that on mute.' The way this was going, we might as well have curled up in the laundry room next to the damn thing. Except most of the floor was awash with a puppy's bodily fluids.

'Just checking,' said El. She turned off the sound, which was a relief. I mean it wasn't just that the sound was annoying. It was kind of pitiful as well.

'You're keeping the screen on?' I asked.

'Yeah,' said El in the tone of voice that implied I was painfully slow on the uptake. 'I have to be sure she's okay. What if she gets into trouble in the night?'

What trouble could you get into in a locked laundry room? Choke on a towel? There was no point in saying anything.

It looked like I wasn't going to get much sleep that night. I'm sensitive to light when I should be sleeping. I can't even stand it if there's a charge light glowing on my bedside cabinet. Elise's phone shone like a lighthouse beacon.

El and I talked. We talked about her parents and my parents and the dog and the court case and England and we didn't make much progress with any of those subjects. Not that we expected to. I think I finally dropped off to sleep around two in the morning.

El woke me at about two thirty by thrusting a phone screen into my face.

'She's fallen asleep,' she said. 'Isn't she cute?'

'I hate you, Elise,' I mumbled.

Dad texted when he and Mr Lee were on their way to pick me up.

Mr Carmichael had made El and me a huge breakfast, which neither of us ate, El because she wanted to take the dog for a walk before school and me because I thought I would throw up anything other than water. I wasn't even confident about the water. After our non-breakfast, Elise's dad piled her and the dog into his car to drive her to school, while Mrs C took their other car to her workplace in the city. I was told I was welcome to stay in the house until Mr Carmichael returned – he worked from home and had apparently made a promise to El that he would let the dog roam the back garden and keep a close eye on her. It was either that or El was going to wag school forever.

I thanked her parents but said I'd rather wait for Dad outside. I needed to move and I needed fresh air. So I stood on the pavement in front of Elise's house and watched as people went about their business – kids going to school, cars passing, the occasional person with a briefcase on their way to the train station, people walking their dogs. It was a clear Melbourne morning. A few clouds littered the sky but didn't interfere with the early sun. It was a day where you feel glad to be alive. It was a day that seemed to dismiss human drama as silly and pointless. One more day in the almost endless cycle of days past and those still to come. Dramas come and go but time steps on and doesn't care.

I took a deep breath. I didn't normally go in for philosophising, especially philosophy that even to my own mind appeared childish and clichéd. But I'd had little sleep and my thoughts were sluggish and confused. I thought I should probably forgive myself.

Dad and his lawyer were a few minutes late, but that was okay. We were down for a nine forty-five hearing and we had to be there at least thirty minutes before that. There was plenty of time, but maybe not enough for me. Now that the moment had arrived I wanted to postpone the judgement for as long as possible.

Dad and Mr Lee were both upbeat as we drove to the court. Apart from asking how I was feeling, neither of them wanted to talk about what the day held for us, and I was okay with that as well. It took ten minutes to get from the car park to the courthouse. Mr Lee wheeled himself into the lifts and we went up to level 6 of the Law Courts building on William Street. Mum and her lawyer were already there, sitting on chairs in a corridor by court number 6B. They stood when we approached and Mum gave me a big hug. I was introduced to Ms Morgan, Mum's lawyer, who told me she was very pleased to meet me. Mum and Dad shook hands, as did the lawyers. I don't really know what I'd been expecting, but this was like being in a doctor's waiting room and unexpectedly bumping into old friends.

While Mr Lee told someone we had arrived, Mum took the opportunity to whisper into my ear.

'Whatever happens, we both love you. You know that, don't you?'

I did. Of course I did. But it was good to hear it anyway.

We waited for what seemed like forever. Mr Lee told me that the hearing would probably be finalised by three thirty that afternoon. Apparently Dad had an appointment at the hospital and it couldn't be rescheduled, but it wouldn't matter. There weren't any witnesses as such and it was simply a matter of presenting each side's respective cases, neither of which was complicated. Mum had agreed to finish early, if things didn't pan out as quickly as anticipated, so Dad could get to the hospital in time. The one thing no one knew was whether the judge would make a judgement that day or bring us back at a later date after thinking it all over.

'Unlikely,' said Mr Lee. 'I think this is being dealt with as a matter of urgency. We should know today, tomorrow at the latest.'

But it was past ten o'clock when we were finally brought into the courtroom by an unsmiling official who reminded us to turn off our mobile phones. Last night, in the hour of sleep I'd finally managed to get, I'd dreamed of oak panelling, a raised dais for the judge with the Australian coat of arms above her head, a witness box and a set of tables where counsel could sit. I was prepared to put this down to watching too many legal dramas on TV, but as it turned out my dreams and reality matched almost exactly.

My father, Mr Lee and I sat at the bar tables to the left, while Mum and her lawyer sat to the right. Each lawyer took documents from their briefcases and placed them on the table.

The court official, who'd been doing something at the front of the room, stood and told us to stand, Judge Catherine Hood presiding. A woman came in through a door to the left of the dais and made her way to the leather seat in the centre, right below the Australian coat of arms. She sat, put on a pair of glasses and picked up a sheaf of papers.

We sat. I wanted to laugh and it was an effort to keep it in. Partly this was down to jangling nerves, but mainly it was because the judge wasn't wearing a wig. Why wasn't she wearing a wig? If I was a judge I'd wear a wig all the time. I'd wear it in bed, in the shower. What was her problem? The thought made me giggle and heads snapped towards me. The judge looked up and her eyes roamed the courtroom before settling on me.

'Hello,' she said. 'You must be Caitlyn Carson. I'm delighted to meet you. I'm Judge Hood, but you can call me Your Honour.' And she gave a grin to show she wasn't taking herself too seriously. I relaxed. I could feel the tension flowing from me. She was just a person. And from what everyone had told me, she was on my side.

'Thank you, Your Honour,' I said. Then I remembered I should have stood, so I did and then sat again because I'd finished speaking. What an idiot.

'I'm interested in who everyone else is,' said the judge. 'Let's start with the Applicant and her counsel. Please introduce yourselves.'

Mum and her lawyer stood, gave their names and then sat down again. The judge turned towards my table.

'And the Respondent and his counsel?'

Dad and I stood.

'Michael Gareth Carson, Your Honour,' said Dad.

Mr Lee gave his name.

The judge glanced down at her papers.

'And no independent children's lawyer has been appointed for Miss Carson, I understand.'

'That's correct, Your Honour,' said Mr Lee. 'I am representing both Miss Carson and her father. This has been agreed to by the Applicant and her counsel.'

'Excellent.' The judge took off her glasses and linked her fingers together. 'The affidavits submitted are all in order, so I suggest we proceed with this hearing. Ms Morgan, if you could briefly outline the case for the Applicant I would be most grateful.'

Mum's lawyer stood.

'Thank you, Your Honour. This is really a very simple matter. The Applicant, Ms Lois Houseman, is applying for a court order allowing her to take her daughter, Caitlyn Rose Carson, to live in England with the Applicant's new partner.' The lawyer didn't pace up and down, but just stood behind the lectern and delivered her speech with little or no emotion. At least my television dramas had added some excitement when lawyers argued. This was like a business meeting that no one found very interesting. 'The Applicant asked permission from the Respondent, but this permission was not forthcoming. Hence the reluctant decision to seek judgement in the Federal Circuit Court, Your Honour. This is a step the Applicant wished to avoid at all costs.'

The judge turned to Mr Lee.

'Is there any part of this that you would challenge, Mr Lee?' she said.

'That is an accurate summation, Your Honour,' said Mr Lee. 'Though I'd like to point out that the Respondent, too, wished to avoid legal action. As we shall argue later, Caitlyn Carson herself has very strong views on where she would like to live and these wishes are incompatible with her mother's desires.'

'I see,' said the judge. 'Well, okay. Let's get to it. Ms Morgan, you have only two witnesses, the Applicant herself and a police officer who was in charge of a road accident involving the Applicant's ex-husband and her daughter. Is that correct?'

'No, Your Honour,' said Mum's lawyer. 'I'm advised by counsel for the Respondent that the evidence from the police officer is not disputed. We both feel that this case can best be decided after hearing from the parents and the child only. As a result, that witness has not been called.'

'That should simplify things,' said Judge Hood. 'Okay, then. Please call Ms Houseman to the stand.'

Mum looked terrified as she made her way to the witness box. I couldn't blame her. I was terrified on her behalf. She was sworn in and she sat in the chair as if facing execution. The judge leaned forward and smiled.

'Please understand that this is as friendly a process as we can manage, Ms Houseman,' she said. 'We deal with children in this court and as a mother you will know that aggression, anger... conflict are not the best ingredients for a child's peace of mind. No one will attack you. Just tell your story, answer questions honestly and everything will be fine.'

'Thank you, Your Honour,' Mum said, and she seemed to relax a little.

Ms Morgan asked Mum a series of routine questions – her name, address, her relationship to me, that kind of thing. After a few minutes, we got down to business.

'Ms Houseman,' said Ms Morgan, 'please tell us the custody and access arrangements for your child after your divorce.'

Mum cleared her throat.

'Well, we agreed – my ex-husband and I – that it would be in Caitlyn's best interests to live with me and have visitation rights to her father every fortnight.'

'This was agreed without a court order. Is that correct?'

'Yes. We had an amicable divorce and both of us felt this was a good arrangement for our daughter. We wanted to avoid the unpleasantness of court.' Mum turned to the judge. 'No offence, Your Honour.'

'None taken, I assure you,' said Judge Hood.

'Why did you think it was in your daughter's best interests to live with you, rather than her father?' Ms Morgan asked.

Mum bowed her head and thought for a long time.

'Caitlyn was six years old,' she said finally. 'She would have night terrors, occasionally wetting the bed.' This was news to me. I remembered nothing of that. Mum, thankfully, moved on. '. . . she would always call out for me. For a long time I was the only one who could comfort her. And I know this sounds sexist, but I think a child's place is with her mother. I couldn't even begin to imagine not having Caitlyn with me.'

'And Caitlyn's father agreed with all of this?'

'Yes.'

Mum's lawyer was in no hurry. She took Mum through all the details of my upbringing, my schooling, trips to the doctor when I was ill, even a visit to the emergency department of our local hospital when I'd had what seemed like an asthma attack. Mum was being shown for what she was – a good, conscientious mother who would do anything to protect her child.

'About a year after your divorce, you found another partner. Is that correct, Ms Houseman? A Mr Sam Ellis?'

'Yes.'

'Please describe the relationship between your partner and your daughter.'

And Mum did. In detail. She talked about how Sam had made it very clear that he did not want to be a father substitute, how he had come along to parent/teacher evenings when my father couldn't make it (and with my father's permission), picked me up from school on many occasions and generally behaved like a sensitive stepdad. I found myself nodding sometimes and had to stop myself. I couldn't imagine that would be helping our case. Finally, Mum's lawyer produced a document from Sam in London and the judge read her copy. I read the copy provided to

Dad and Mr Lee. It was a good letter that managed to show his support for me, his determination to look after me as best he could, all without saying anything negative about Dad. He also managed to fit in everything about his job, the fact that he had found accommodation for us in London and that he had checked out possible schools. It was the letter of a responsible person who clearly cared about me.

'I'd like to turn now to your ex-husband and his relationship with Caitlyn,' said Ms Morgan.

'Okay,' said Mum, but she swallowed. So far everything had been civilised and polite. I knew that was about to change.

'Do you have any evidence that Caitlyn's father has been... shall we say, derelict... in his duty of care towards his daughter?'

Mum glanced at us, then turned her head away. She cleared her throat and took a sip of water from the glass in front of her. The silence stretched out for quite a long time.

'Mike Carson loves Cate,' said Mum finally. 'I have never had any doubts about that. He is protective and he goes to considerable efforts to... entertain her during her visits.'

She stopped, took another drink. We all waited. I was glad she'd used Dad's name. All this stuff about biological relationships – mother, father, daughter – was vaguely upsetting, like we had been reduced to facts rather than feelings.

'But . . . I believe that sometimes he does not think through the consequences of his actions as a parent should.'

'Please explain.'

And Mum went through the accident, how Dad had issued specific instructions that I should get into the well at the back of the car, that I should *not* wear a seatbelt when he was driving. The judge interrupted at this point and asked for an explanation; Mum told her a little bit about the role-playing Dad and I did when I was at his house. Judge Hood frowned and made a note on the pad in front of her.

'Afterwards I talked to a specialist at the hospital,' Mum continued, 'and he mentioned something about immature personality disorder, that maybe Mike . . .'

Mr Lee raised his hand, but then obviously thought better of it and put it down again. He leaned over and whispered something in my father's ear. Dad nodded.

Mum's lawyer then got her to talk about why she thought I would be better off in England with her and Sam. This was clearly a topic they had gone over, because Mum was fluent and confident. She talked about adolescence and how a mother was best suited to navigate troubling times and guide a child towards adulthood. Mum said that Dad didn't have a partner and therefore I would be deprived of a mother figure who could understand the specific issues that girls faced in a very important phase of their physical and emotional development. She talked about financial security, the educational and cultural opportunities that would be presented to me and how I would be able to visit Dad regularly, thus providing me with opportunities to maintain my relationship with him and keep contact with friends here. It was all pretty impressive. If I was the judge, I knew which way I would be leaning.

Mr Lee must've understood what I was thinking. What had Dad said? My thoughts were always written on my face? Mr Lee patted my hand and whispered to me.

'We haven't had our turn yet.'

It was time for him to cross-examine Mum. He wheeled his chair to the front of the court.

'Ms Houseman. You mentioned a psychiatric disorder in relation to your ex-husband. Immature personality disorder, I think it was.'

'Yes.'

'But you are a schoolteacher, yes? Not a qualified psychiatrist?'

'That's correct.'

'And you have not called a qualified psychiatrist to give testimony today?'

'No. Caitlyn's father refused to be evaluated.'

'Not surprisingly.' Mr Lee moved on quickly. 'So it's just your *opinion* that Caitlyn's father is sometimes immature? Would that be fair?'

'I suppose so.'

'Do you dance with your daughter, Ms Houseman?'

'I'm sorry?'

'I believe that occasionally you and Caitlyn dance to music at home. She tells me you are particularly good at . . .' He took a piece of paper from where it had been resting in his lap, skimmed for the right place. 'Twerking, I believe it's called.'

Mum blushed. 'Yes. It's a bit silly, but good fun.'

'It sounds it,' said Mr Lee in a tone of voice that clearly doubted it. 'So a bit of immaturity can be a good thing sometimes, when an adult deals with a child. Getting down to the child's level, as it were. Would you agree?'

'Yes.'

'Not a disorder, then?'

I wanted Mr Lee to move on. He'd made his point.

'No,' said Mum.

'Okay. Let's move on to the accident, Ms Houseman. You are not arguing that Mr Carson intended Caitlyn to come to harm?'

'Of course not.'

'He made a mistake.'

'A very serious one.'

Mr Lee waited a couple of beats. 'One that might have had serious *consequences*, but a single mistake nonetheless.'

'I suppose so.'

'Have you ever made a mistake in your parenting, Ms Houseman?'

'I beg your pardon?'

'Didn't Caitlyn break a finger when she was eight, falling from a swing in a children's play area while you were supervising her?'

Mum wanted to squirm. She could see where this was

going. Dad got to his feet, made to step towards Mr Lee and then obviously worried that he was breaking some law, or protocol at the very least. The judge smiled at him.

'You may talk to your lawyer, Mr Carson,' she said.

'Thank you, Your Honour.'

Dad stepped forward and whispered into Mr Lee's ear. The lawyer nodded and Dad returned to his seat.

'There's no need to answer that question, Ms Houseman,' said Mr Lee. 'In fact, I don't have any more questions. Thank you.'

The judge called for a lunch break and left the courtroom. Mum smiled at me, but left with her lawyer as we collected our things. It was clear that Dad wanted to talk to Mr Lee, but also clear that he didn't want to do it in front of me. So I left and went down the stairs, stepped out into the sunshine.

I checked my phone. I had twelve texts from Elise, all of them asking in various ways how it was going. I looked at the time. Still forty minutes before lunch break at school. So I texted her back. *Grim. Serious. Not fun. But necessary. Will ring when done.*

And then suddenly I knew that I didn't want to witness the rest of the case, where Dad would be giving evidence and Mum's lawyer would try to punch holes in his character. I knew what was going to be said. Was it possible for someone to come and fetch me when it was my turn on the witness stand? I knew I wanted to give evidence. I had spent considerable time preparing my statement and I wanted it to be heard. But I could do without the rest.

Turns out everyone was happy for me to sit out the afternoon's proceedings, though both Mum and Dad insisted I sit on the chairs outside the courtroom. This was partly so I would be there when called for, but mainly because it wouldn't reflect well on either of them for me to be wandering around Melbourne unsupervised while they argued they were totally responsible parents. At least I could ring El during her lunchtime. She wanted all the details but I just gave her the broad brushstrokes. I'd been through it once. I didn't want to go through it again.

So I sat, played on my phone, got up, paced a while, sat down again, took a bite of the sandwich that Dad had bought for me. Put all of that on repeat.

Then the door opened and the court official beckoned me. Even then, he didn't smile. I walked in. Everyone looked at me as I made my way to the witness box. Performance time.

Oh shit.

# CHAPTER FIFTEEN

★

Mr Lee brought over the sheaf of papers that was my statement. I'd thought about memorising it like a movie script, but decided against it. For one thing, this wasn't a movie. Secondly, I worried I'd forget my thread and dribble to a stop. The papers felt like a lifeline.

Mr Lee smiled and then went back to his place next to Dad, who gave me a thumbs up. Mum did the same and I almost laughed. They had so much in common. Why had they fallen out of love? It was a tragedy. All of this was a tragedy.

I cleared my throat and adjusted the microphone.

'Your Honour,' I said. Then I paused, cleared my throat again and wiped sweat from my forehead. Where had that come from? It wasn't even vaguely warm in the courtroom. I looked down at the first sheet. 'Your Honour, I was six years old when I saw a unicorn.

'I want to tell you about it, but I also want to tell you

what happened in the six months before I saw it. Some of my memories may not be trustworthy because I was only six and things get confused at that age. But I remember some things and I certainly remember the atmosphere of that time, the texture of it. It was harsh and scratchy. It was dark and there was a weight, as if something was pressing down on all of us: my mother, my father and me. Looking back on that time I see us all as figures bent and buckled by worry.'

Was I reading too fast? I took a deep breath and tried to slow everything down.

'My parents split for reasons that have never been clear to me. I haven't asked because . . . well, sometimes it's best not to look too closely into closets for the skeletons and other grisly stuff that might leap out. They talked to me about what would happen after they separated because that's what good parents do and, until this day, no one has ever suggested that either my mother or my father are anything other than brilliant parents.'

I looked up then. Mum and Dad were both smiling.

'But I don't remember the *whole* conversation. What I do remember is waking up one day in my bed and *feeling* my father's absence from the house. Until that moment I didn't know you could feel an absence. I went down to breakfast and Mum poured out some cornflakes for me and I put in the milk and she sprinkled in the sugar because I always put in too much if I did it myself. And we pretended everything was normal, that the father-shaped hole in my life simply didn't exist.

'I think it was about a month before I went for my first weekend with Dad. He had to find somewhere to live and get things organised for a six-year-old girl. But he called me every day. I was really excited when I packed my bag that first time on a Friday evening. It felt like a holiday. I put in all the normal stuff – pyjamas, toothbrush and toothpaste (Mum insisted on that in case Dad forgot), but I also put in my favourite toys. At that time, Dad didn't even have a television because the divorce meant Mum and Dad were both broke and he had to save up for it. And Mum drove me to his house because they only had the one car and Mum got it because she needed it to take me to school. When I got to Dad's place, though, I realised that Mum shouldn't have worried. He had bought all the things I would need – the toothbrush, the paste, the shower gel, the shampoo and conditioner I always used, the shower puff and toys... so many toys. I think he'd got most of them, if not all, from a charity shop, because some things had bits missing and there was a rip in one doll's dress. I was six. I didn't care. It was all strange and exciting and it felt so good to have him back in my life. He read me a story that night. He still reads me a story at night and I'm nearly fourteen. It's a routine and we like our routines.'

I paused again. Dad wiped something from his eye. Mum was apparently studying the wood grain of her table.

'On the Saturday, Dad got me all dressed up in warm clothes. It was winter and I suppose it was chilly out.

I don't remember that exactly, but I know I was wearing a scarf and I seem to remember seeing my breath mist the air. We went for a walk in a forest. I don't know which forest and I can't remember whether we walked there or if we took a bus. Those things are lost. But we didn't see other people. There was a faint walking track and there were lots of trees and I noticed how the sunshine filtered through them and made everything seem mysterious and fairytale like. Sometimes there was birdsong and sometimes things scuttled in the undergrowth and made me scared. But this I do remember, Your Honour. This is burned in my memory.

'I walked up a slight incline and there was a bank ahead. When I got to the top I saw a clearing down below. And in that clearing was a unicorn. It was all by itself and it turned its head as I stood there and looked at me. It was pure white and on its forehead was a horn of burnished silver. I don't know how long we stared at each other, but it seemed a long time. I think I was holding my breath. The unicorn pawed at the ground and then turned and trotted away. Not scared. Not in a great rush. Moving quietly and purposefully. It moved between trees and then it was gone and I could breathe again.

'I turned and asked my father if he had seen it too.

'He had.

'"But unicorns don't exist," I said. I might have been only six but I knew that unicorns don't exist. I began to have doubts about Father Christmas the year after that.

'"Who says they don't exist?" asked my father.

'"Everyone," I replied.

'"Maybe everyone is wrong, Caitlyn. Did that not occur to you?"

'It hadn't.

'"Close your eyes, Cate," he continued. I did. "Now I want you to think about what you just saw. Can you do that? Can you build that picture in your mind? As many details as you possibly can. The way the light fell, the colour of the unicorn's coat, the way its mane moved as it turned, the shape and colour of its horn. Can you fix all of those things in your mind? Can you see it again now, Cate?"

'I could. Although my eyes were closed I could see it all again. I nodded.

'"It's there in your head now, Cate," said Dad. "And if it's in your head it must be real. It will always be real as long as you remember it."

'"It's a miracle, Daddy," I said. When I opened my eyes, Dad was kneeling down in front of me, his eyes on my level.

'"It is," he said. "It's a miracle and we both believe in miracles, don't we?"

'I nodded. I did then. I do now, Your Honour.

'I don't know how my father arranged for that unicorn to be in that forest at that particular time. I can guarantee the small horse he used wasn't hurt by having something attached to its forehead. My father couldn't be cruel to animals. If I think about it now, then I can probably guess. He paid someone for the use of the horse, he arranged its transport to that location so that I would stumble across a miracle he had designed. He had made a theatre, he had written a script and he'd arranged for the actors to be in their places. It was the most amazing thing any child could have witnessed. I get goosebumps even now, thinking about it.'

I took another sip of water. The silence was overpowering. I was glad to carry on speaking just to shatter it.

'There were little miracles nearly every time I stayed with my father after that. Oh, most of them weren't spectacular – bread and butter miracles, Your Honour. A metre-wide web with a golden orb-weaving spider at its centre as we walked through the botanical gardens. A new ice-cream shop that had just opened and we stumbled across. A street magician doing the most amazing tricks. Buskers who seemed always to sing my favourite songs, as if someone with insider information had briefed them before we showed up. Mixed in with these were some "ordinary" adventures. Things like a balloon ride in the early Saturday morning, a houseboat he had booked, theatre trips where we had front seats. But then there were others that were like the unicorn adventure. I saw a Tasmanian tiger once, Your Honour. It ran across the road as we were driving in Gippsland. I still have no idea how he arranged that. And I don't want to know, to be honest. Just recently we saw some UFOs in formation in the early hours of the morning, just outside Melbourne. Our car was lit up by one, fixed in the beam of something from another planet. How much does it cost, Your

Honour, to arrange for drones to appear way out in the middle of nowhere? How do you go about arranging that, even if you can afford it? Probably a lot harder than paying a couple of buskers to turn up at St Kilda beach and sing a song to me.'

I sat up straight in the chair. Out of the corner of my eye I could see the judge leaning towards me, concentrating. But I kept my focus on Dad.

'My father is a director of miracles, Your Honour. He has spent countless hours arranging his theatre. I don't want to think how much money he's spent on them. He would doubtless say that doesn't matter. The last miracle he'd arranged was a simple weekend away in a hotel. A cheap hotel, it seems, but that was part of the narrative. We were going to be cast in a thriller. Shadowy people, maybe from the underworld, maybe from the authorities, were after us and we had to keep ourselves alive. He hired a car – Dad was always careful about realism – and picked me up from school. And this is where he made his mistake. It would have been better if I'd just got into the front seat and put on the wig for my disguise there. But Dad wanted more drama. He told me to get into the well at the back. But I think he knew this was a bad idea. He was just about to pull over and get me into the front seat when that vehicle ploughed into us. A million to one chance, really.'

Now I turned slightly to face Mum and in particular her lawyer.

'But here is something to think about. That four-wheel drive hit us as it came through red lights at speed. It hit us smack in the passenger door. Dad was severely injured. Lying in the back of the car, I was hurt but not as severely as Dad. It's not unreasonable to believe that if I had been in the passenger seat I would have been killed instantly. I genuinely believe my father's mistake saved my life. This was a miracle he hadn't scripted.

'Your Honour, I understand the counter argument to this. My father failed in a duty of care and although this might have had accidental positive outcomes, it doesn't change the fact he failed in that duty of care. But if you rule that my mother can take me away from my father, then it seems that this is one huge and unreasonable price to pay for one mistake in thirteen years.

'I also understand that it is *my* best interests that will govern your decision in this case. It is hard for me to argue that my mother has not done her very best for my wellbeing. She has clothed me, fed me, protected me and loved me. My mother once said – and I cannot quite remember her exact words, since we were both very upset at the time – that she and her partner, Sam, had dealt with the dull, everyday responsibilities of bringing up a child while my father had the luxury of playing games with me. She implied that he was trying to get me to prefer his company over hers simply by refusing to deal with the unglamourous side of parenting. But while my mother fed my body, my father fed my imagination.

'We have heard arguments that these "games" demonstrated his immaturity. Some very famous people disagree with that view. Albert Einstein once said that logic will get you from A to B but imagination will take you everywhere. George Bernard Shaw was of the opinion that we don't stop playing because we grow old; we grow old because we stop playing. My father and I have never stopped playing. I have had some success as a writer, Your Honour. I believe this is a direct result of my father giving my imagination permission to flourish. Yet it has been implied in this court that somehow this is evidence of a psychological problem. But here's what another famous person, celebrated for his supposed craziness, thought about this. Robin Williams, the American comedian and actor, once said, "You're only given a little spark of madness. You mustn't lose it."'

Now I turned towards the judge.

'Your Honour, I don't want to lose my little spark.

'My mother has two enduring loves in her life: me and her partner, Sam. My father has only me. Now it has been argued that his lack of a partner is a reason why judgement should be made against him. Yet I know that my father has deliberately kept away from relationships that might compete with ours. All he wanted when we were together – a few days every couple of weeks – was that nothing could come between us. He was one hundred per cent focused on me. It would be a strange logic to say that this is a failing. It isn't. It's a huge sacrifice that he has made willingly.

'Finally, I would like to make this point. My father has not been well since the accident and he needs support, both emotionally and physically. He doesn't have a partner to provide that support and he needs me. Mum, I repeat, has Sam. I could go to visit them whenever they wished. Because my place is here, Your Honour. With both my parents, if possible. But that can't happen. So given I am *forced* to choose, I choose my father.'

I addressed my last sentence directly to the judge.

'I humbly request that you honour my wishes in your ruling. Thank you.'

I sat still. I really wanted to get the hell out of that chair, out of that spotlight, but I knew that I might have to answer questions from Mum's lawyer, maybe even Mr Lee. I just hoped it wouldn't take too long.

'That's quite a speech, young lady,' said the judge. 'Well done. Ms Morgan, do you have any questions?'

Mum's lawyer stood.

'Just a couple, Your Honour. Very brief.' She looked at me. 'I'd like to add my congratulations, Caitlyn,' she said. 'I can see how you've enjoyed success as a writer. But tell me. Do you think imagination is something you either have or don't have?'

I must have looked puzzled because she tried again.

'Can you *learn* imagination?'

'I don't think it's something you can learn, exactly,' I replied. 'But I do believe it's something that flourishes when properly tended.'

'Well expressed,' said Ms Morgan. 'But your mother does this as well, doesn't she? Play games, I mean? There's your dancing sessions and she takes you to movies and the theatre. You all dress up for Halloween, isn't that so?'

'Yes.'

'So encouraging your imagination is something that both parents have done, yes? Not just your father?'

'My dad more than my mum,' I said.

'I'm sure,' said Mum's lawyer. 'But that's all he has to worry about, isn't it? Whereas your mum has to look after all the other stuff as well as feeding your imagination.'

'I'm not sure about that.'

'Never mind,' said Ms Morgan. 'I have no other questions, Your Honour.'

The judge looked at Mr Lee.

'Nothing from me, Your Honour.'

'Then you can stand down, Caitlyn. Thank you for your testimony.'

I was glad to sit next to Dad again. He patted my knee.

The judge glanced at her watch.

'I believe this is a good time to adjourn for the day,' she said. 'Please reconvene at nine thirty am tomorrow in this courtroom when I will deliver my judgement.'

The court official stood.

'This court is now adjourned,' he said. 'All stand.'

We stood until the judge left the room. Then Dad went over to Mum and shook her hand. I joined them. Mum smiled at me.

'Okay, Cate,' she said. 'Let's get you home.' She turned back to Dad. 'I suppose it's okay for me to bring Cate here with me tomorrow, is it, Mike?'

'Of course,' said Dad. 'It's all over now, whatever the decision, so it really doesn't make any difference.'

He ruffled my hair. 'And apparently we're both brilliant parents.'

'It seems that way,' said Mum. She put a hand on my shoulder. 'We'll do takeaway tonight, Cate. I think we all deserve it.' She turned to Dad. 'You could join us if you want to, Mike.'

Dad smiled.

'I think that might be a bridge too far,' he said. 'Thank you, but I'll leave you to it. And see you both in the morning.'

'You didn't tell me what happened when you spent the weekends with your dad.'

We went for Indian takeaway this time, which meant I didn't have to embarrass myself with chopsticks. I ordered butter chicken with garlic naan as always. I love spicy food, but too much chilli upsets my stomach. Not so with Mum. She sometimes bemoans the fact that it's difficult to get a vegetable vindaloo, so she ordered a paneer chilli masala and asked them to ramp up the heat content.

'No,' I said. 'But then I don't tell him what we do at home with Sam.'

Mum nodded and speared a cube of cheese. 'It's a shame you feel the need to keep secrets from both your parents.'

I thought about this. It was an angle I'd never considered before.

'I don't think about it as keeping secrets,' I said finally. 'More protecting worlds.'

'One of which will be closed tomorrow,' Mum said. 'To all intents and purposes.'

I'd thought about this. Of course I had. But I still felt a lump come to my throat hearing it expressed as bluntly as that.

'Yes,' I said.

'I learned a lot today,' said Mum. 'Your statement was . . . well, it was wonderful, Cate. I don't know what I thought happened when you went to your dad's. I guess I assumed you'd be doing what you do here. You know, bit of homework, maybe watch TV, talk to Elise for hours on the phone. I figured the world there was no different from the world here.' She tore herself a chunk of naan bread. 'Now I know better.'

'Do you still resent Dad for . . . I can't remember how you expressed it, but something like having the easier job as a parent?'

'No. If anything, what I learned today was that maybe *my* role was easier. Your father gave of himself every second he was with you, it seems. I can't claim that.' Mum put her fork down and rubbed at her forehead. 'It's easier to wash your school uniform than it is to create miracles.'

'I need both,' I said.

Mum laughed. 'Well, there's no point rocking up to a miracle if you're in dirty clothes,' she said. Then the smile vanished as quickly as it had come. 'What do you think the judge will say tomorrow, Cate?'

'I don't know. Seriously, no idea.' I hadn't heard Dad's testimony, of course, so it was hard for me to come to any informed conclusion. 'But it would be a brave decision to go against you.'

'Brave?'

'We're meant to believe that men and women are treated equally under the law, but that's not right, Mum, and you know it. Women still earn less than men. Men dominate positions of power.'

'Yup. It's a man's world,' said Mum. 'Always has been.'

'But the judge is a woman,' I said.

'Which means she will be fair and not be biased by gender, as many men are.'

'Maybe,' I said. 'But she will also know that I was a part of your body for nine months, that you gave birth to me, breastfed me and shared – still share – a bond unlike any other. I don't think a man would have that kind of... understanding. That's what I mean by brave.'

Mum took up another forkful of curry, put it down again. She seemed tired and defeated.

'I was confident about winning this, Cate,' she said. 'Until today. Until I heard your dad speak and until I heard you speak. Now I'm not so sure.'

'We'll know soon enough.'

'I was...' Mum picked up the rest of the bread, shredded it between her fingers and dropped the mess back onto the plate. 'Never mind. Are you done?'

'What were you going to say?'

'It doesn't matter.'

'It does. What were you going to say?'

Mum sighed. 'If you and your father win . . . if you're staying here in Australia, then I'm staying too. That's all.'

There are times when your emotions ambush you. You don't know when and sometimes you don't even know why. It just happens, which I guess is in the nature of ambushes. There was a hot coal of anger deep within me that I hadn't even realised was there, and Mum's words had fanned it.

'What? Are you kidding? Tell me you're kidding.'

Mum met my eyes and there was no longer defeat in there. It had been replaced with steeliness.

'I cannot leave you here and go to England, Cate. It's as simple as that. If you're staying here, then so am I. Okay, we'll probably have to renegotiate access and official custody status and . . .'

I'd sworn not to cry and I didn't, but it was close.

'So what was all this about then, Mum?' I yelled. 'This court case that I seem to remember you made me feel guilty about. What happened to *my daughter would be better off with me and Sam in England*, huh? Shit, what happened to you and Sam, the love of your life, apparently?'

'Don't swear, Cate.'

'And what happens then, Mum?' The words were pouring from me, an undammable flood. 'Sam comes back to Australia and I've screwed up his career? Or he doesn't come home and I've screwed up your life? Well, thanks for nothing, Mum. I'll just carry that guilt with me, yeah?'

I might have banned myself from crying, but Mum hadn't. She wailed.

'I *can't* go off without you, Cate.' She wiped at a small trail of snot creeping from her left nostril. 'I'm not trying to make you feel guilty. I'm just telling you what I can't do. I can't leave you. Do you understand?'

'Yes,' I said. 'I understand. I understand that if I win, then everyone loses.'

And I got up from the table and went to my bedroom, slammed the door. The nightmare wasn't ending. It seemed it was just beginning. I got into bed and it was barely seven thirty. I thought I would never sleep, but almost immediately sleep found me.

I didn't dream. That was good.

# CHAPTER SIXTEEN

★

I had four missed calls from Elise and about sixteen text messages. Most of those were pictures and videos of the puppy doing puppy things. It was too early to call her back – five thirty in the morning – but I messaged her with most of what had been going on in my miserable life. She knew I was returning to court today – I'd sent a quick text when I was in the car with Mum on the way back the previous day – but I promised I would ring as soon as there was a judgement.

I took a chair into the backyard and watched as dawn slowly blushed the sky. I hadn't realised there was so much bird noise in our suburb, though at a quarter to six traffic was already building up and drowning out their songs. I couldn't remember the full extent of my anger from the previous night. I couldn't even fully understand it. If Dad won, then I would have both my parents with me. In a sense, nothing would have changed. What had

I said in my statement? *My place is here in Australia, with both my parents, if possible.* Now that was possible. So why was I angry? I knew some of the reasons, but the full explanation was just out of my grasp.

Of course, if Mum won, then I'd be losing Dad. Another reason why the judgement today was going to be life-changing, in one way or another.

Mum was up by six thirty and she made me a breakfast of scrambled eggs. We didn't talk much, but what we said was polite, even affectionate. Then we got dressed in our best clothes and headed off to the courthouse. We were super early. The judge had said nine thirty but we were outside the court building just before eight thirty. We couldn't even get in, so we just hung around in front like confused tourists. Mum's lawyer arrived with Mr Lee at nine and we trooped into the building and up to level 6.

I checked the time on my phone. Nine fifteen and no sign of Dad. I tried ringing him but it went straight to messages. Nine twenty and the court official, looking even grimmer than yesterday, called us into the courtroom. No Dad but also no judge. We sat in our respective seats and waited. Nine twenty-five.

At nine twenty-eight, the door opened and I felt a wave of relief. I turned in my chair, but it was a stranger in the doorway. She looked around, apologised and left. The court official stood.

'All rise. This court is now in session, Judge Hood presiding.'

The judge entered from the door to the left of the front bench, sat beneath the coat of arms and opened up a folder. I took the opportunity to whisper to Mr Lee.

'Did Dad say he was going to be late?'

Mr Lee shook his head. 'I've not heard from him, Caitlyn, since he said he'd make his own way here. Have you tried calling?'

Even though we weren't supposed to use our phones in court, I put mine on my lap and tried calling Dad again. The phone was on mute, but I'd obviously be able to tell if he answered. He didn't. There were no text messages either. I put the phone away, just as the judge looked up at us. I felt like a naughty kid in school.

'Good morning,' said Judge Hood.

'Good morning, Your Honour,' said Mr Lee. 'Unfortunately, the Respondent, Mr Carson, appears to be delayed. I apologise on his behalf and crave your indulgence for a few moments.'

For the first time, the judge seemed to be annoyed.

'We all managed to get here on time, Mr Lee,' she said. 'I'm not best pleased that your client didn't. I am prepared . . .'

But she didn't get a chance to finish. The door burst open and Dad came in, flushed and sweaty. He stopped immediately inside and bowed his head to the judge.

'My apologies, Your Honour,' he said.

The judge was still a bit pissy.

'Accepted, Mr Carson. Now please sit. My schedule is very busy today.'

But Dad didn't sit. He grabbed Mr Lee by the arm and whispered in his ear. Something was wrong. I'd never seen Dad so agitated. I mean, okay, he was late and that had probably stressed him out, but this was next level. Mr Lee turned to the judge.

'Begging your pardon, Your Honour, but my client wishes to have a quick word with me. Outside, Your Honour.'

'Very well.' Judge Hood's tone was icy. 'But a couple of minutes only, Mr Lee. And you should know that I am not best pleased by these delays.'

I stood to go outside as well. I had no idea what was going on, but I wasn't going to wait to find out. Dad stopped me.

'Stay here, Cate.'

'What? No.'

'Stay here!'

And then they were gone. Mr Lee stopped at the door, turned his chair around and bowed his head to the judge, but Dad was already outside. He sure wasn't doing himself any favours with the court today. I looked at Mum, who spread her hands in a *What?* gesture. I shrugged.

They were gone for a couple of minutes. When they came back in, neither met my eyes. Dad sat, but Mr Lee moved to the front of the court.

'Your Honour,' he said. 'My client informs me that he is withdrawing his objections to the Applicant's case. He apologises to the court and all parties for wasting their time. He will sign, without delay, the relevant documentation for his daughter's emigration to the United Kingdom and he will pay the legal costs for the Applicant.'

There was a stunned silence. Everyone's eyes went to my father. He simply looked at his fingers interlocked on his lap. It was the judge who broke the silence.

'Mr Carson,' she said. Dad looked up. 'I wish to hear this from your own lips. You are withdrawing your objection to your daughter leaving the country to live in England. Is this correct?'

Dad stood.

'Yes, Your Honour.'

'And this is your final decision?'

'Yes, Your Honour.'

The judge sighed. 'Very well . . .'

Then I found myself standing.

'No,' I yelled. 'This can't be happening. What about me? What about my wishes?' I turned to Dad. 'What's going on, Dad?'

The judge was altogether gentler with me.

'Please sit, Caitlyn,' she said. 'I understand you're upset, but please sit.' I did. 'I'm afraid that now your parents are in agreement, your wishes are no longer important. From a legal point of view.' She directed a stern glance towards Mum and then Dad. 'Though I am sure your parents in the future will make every effort to take your feelings into account. But you are a minor, Caitlyn, and therefore not yet in a position to make these kinds of decisions on your own behalf. I'm sorry.'

I tried to stand, but Dad put a hand on my arm.

'All rise.' The court official again. I remained seated. If I was a minor, a child, then I was going to behave as one. If I couldn't stand when I wanted to then I wasn't going to stand when they told me to. But it didn't help. That burning ember of anger inside was flaring. As soon as the judge had left the courtroom, I was in Dad's face.

'What the hell, Dad? Why? Tell me why. I don't understand.'

'I've had time to think, Cate,' said Dad. 'I'm sorry, but I've come to the conclusion that it is in your best interests to be with your mother.'

'Dad, this is crazy. You've had time to think? You hadn't been thinking for the last couple of months, then? Just last night. This doesn't make sense. I want to know what's going on.'

'Nothing is going on, Cate. I just think your mother is right, that's all.'

'You told me you would fight for me. You said that if I wanted to stay in Australia you would fight for me. What happened to that?'

'I changed my mind, Cate. I'm sorry.'

'You're sorry? That's not good enough.'

'It will have to be, Cate. I've made up my mind.'

A courtroom is a solemn place. All that wood panelling, the coat of arms, the judge's bench and the witness box and bar tables. The atmosphere. The sense that important decisions are made, outcomes weighed and judged. The learning. The wisdom. None of it was a match for that burning anger. It was no longer an ember. It was a blaze.

'Well, screw you, Dad,' I yelled. I ran to the door, turned and yelled again. 'SCREW YOU.'

I have no idea if anyone tried to follow me as I ran down the stairs and out into William Street. Even if they had, I don't think anyone would have caught me. I had at least thirty years on all of them. I think I went down Little Bourke Street, maybe Elizabeth Street. Cafes, shops, people everywhere and me running, running as if chased by something evil. When I stopped I was in front of the State Library. People lounged on the grass or sat on the steps and benches in front of the array of pillars. I found a spot behind a group of what I guessed were Japanese tourists. My phone, still on silent, buzzed in my hand. I glanced at the screen. Mum. I didn't answer.

Pigeons strutted around me, people chatted or just soaked up the sunshine or took pictures with their phones. No one paid me any attention. So I sat and I sat and people came and people went and pigeons strutted and then strutted some more. I sat and waited until my anger had died down a little. It wasn't a blaze but it wasn't an ember either.

*No crying*, I reminded myself.

I stayed there for probably three or four hours. When I stood my legs and back ached from being in one position for so long. I didn't care. I hopped on a tram to Flinders

Street station. I couldn't stay away forever. It was time to go home. I texted Mum to let her know I was on my way. There were a couple of missed calls from Dad and a couple of texts.

I deleted them.

I really didn't want to go to school, but I also knew my time there was running out. And it stopped me thinking. Anything that stopped me thinking was good.

Elise was someone teetering on the brink of despair, but she kept her balance – for my sake, I think. We tried to talk normally – the dog, the looming divorce at her place, the various rumours and scandals and gossip that were hot topics in the school classrooms and corridors. What we didn't talk about was my imminent departure, a dark presence we thought might just go away if we didn't acknowledge it.

It didn't go away.

I thought of all the things I'd be leaving. Not just people, though they were obviously the most important. But all the other stuff. The Melbourne Cricket Ground (though I'd never been inside, it was still . . . there), that stupid grinning face at Luna Park, the way the wind could make you feel like you were in a fan oven, the four seasons in a day, the people from every corner of the world milling around Elizabeth Street, the weirdos who bailed you up on the train, the smells on Little Bourke Street, the Vic Market with all its food stalls. The trams.

Oh God, the trams. I'd never known anything else. All these things were woven into me. I didn't know who I'd be without them. I didn't want to know.

On the Friday afternoon after the court case, Mo Axon from Blake McDonald Publishers came to my house. Mum had argued strongly that my father should be there for the meeting, but I refused. Mum said I was being childish. I said I didn't care. The way I looked at it, the whole thing was a complete waste of time. Mum wouldn't let me cancel. She said I was spitting the dummy. I said I didn't care.

Mo Axon explained why *Unicorn Girl* was not suitable for publication and why even rewriting and editing wouldn't get it to that place. I just nodded. She also said that she wanted to see whatever I was writing next. I told her I wasn't writing and anyway I would be moving to England in a matter of weeks.

She said that writing from England wasn't a total barrier for an Australian publishing house, but that they published stories with an Australian feel and if I continued writing I should understand that. If London was going to be where my future lay, then English publishers might be the way to go.

'There is a Blake McDonald branch in London,' she said. 'One of the publishers there is a close friend. I will get in touch and let her know you are someone worth nurturing. And please keep on writing, Caitlyn. You have been given a wonderful gift and it would be a tragedy if you didn't use it.'

I nodded. I thanked her. I didn't tell her there were no more stories in me. I just wanted her to go.

The weeks passed all too quickly. My father tried ringing most days, but I wouldn't answer. He texted, but I deleted them without reading. After a couple of weeks the frequency of calls started to dwindle. I think Mum told him I wasn't reading his texts because one day I got an old-fashioned letter. I recognised his handwriting and didn't open it. Mum did everything she could to change my mind. She pleaded. She bullied. She got angry. It didn't matter.

'It's unlike you to be so childish, Cate,' she said.

'I *am* a child,' I said. 'That's why I have no control over my life.'

I put the unopened letter in the bin. I stopped replying to Sam's messages on WhatsApp, even though I knew that none of this was his fault. I became detached from almost everything apart from Elise. I didn't complete any school assignments. What was the point? On my last day of school – a week before the flight to London – my English teacher, Mr Carlisle, organised a party for me. He bought cake and we just messed around and it was desperately sad, but I couldn't find a tear anywhere. Elise tried to get me excited about London, but we both knew she was overcompensating. Her father had moved out and home was better for it, simply because there was no atmosphere of thinly veiled distaste. Her puppy was growing so fast that if you stared at her you could almost see it.

She told me about a conversation she'd had with her mum.

'Don't you think a Saint Bernard is just . . . well, just too big?' her mum had asked.

'No,' said El.

'It's just that I'm a single parent now and the house isn't that big and we live in the suburbs and the dog's destroying the garden and . . .'

'What's your point?'

Her mum apparently waved her hands around in a vague manner.

'Saint Bernards grow to be so huge. They drool, mope around and, to be honest, they break wind in a disgusting fashion all the time.'

'Dad's huge,' El pointed out. 'He drooled, moped around and could fart for Australia. Still can. It's like we just swapped things over.'

'Exactly,' said her mum. 'You see what I'm getting at. How about we sell her and get a Saint Bernard crossed with something like a cocker spaniel? Still cute, but not so . . . huge.'

'How about we don't?'

El knew that her mum couldn't force her. They'd agreed that day in the hospital. Guilt is a powerful thing. From that point on, the subject was closed.

Anyway, the puppy was allowed to stay in her room at night now because El had spent so much time and patience toilet training her. Two days before the flight I slept over at her place. I say *slept* but really we stayed awake all night and talked. Most of the talk was just a way of avoiding proper talk. We agreed that Elise wouldn't come to the airport to see me off. We understood that some things are just too painful. When Mum came to pick me up in the morning, I got into the car and didn't look back. El had closed her front door as soon as I had gone through it.

We tried for coping mechanisms but, to be honest, none of them worked.

Mum told me that Dad was coming to the airport to see us off. I told her that an airport was a public place and I couldn't stop anyone from rocking up.

'I know you're angry, Cate,' said Mum. 'But he is your father. Nothing can alter that. Don't burn bridges that may never be rebuilt.'

I nodded. I knew she was right. I was being stubborn and stupid and none of that could change the outcome. I'd be on that flight whether I hugged Dad or spat in his face. I couldn't see myself doing either.

In the end it was Mum who hugged Dad at the departure gate, for much longer than I would have thought possible. When they finally broke away, Mum was sobbing and Dad wiped a tear from his eye. They'd always been polite in their dealings with each other. Now they parted like lovers, ripped apart by fate and miserable about it.

Then Dad hugged me. I hadn't made any resolutions – though I imagined I'd be cool and distant when the time came to say goodbye – but I reacted without thinking. I hugged him back. I hadn't forgiven him. But I hadn't stopped loving him either. I hadn't realised until that moment.

'I'm sorry,' he said.

'Me too,' I replied.

Love. It has a lot to answer for. Mostly, it is bewildering.

Then Mum and I got on a plane and flew to another world.

# TWO MONTHS LATER

# CHAPTER SEVENTEEN
★

'So is it true that, like, nearly everything in Australia can kill you, know wha' I mean? You know, like animals an' 'at?'

'Oh, yeah,' I replied. 'Most of the wildlife is pretty deadly.' I looked around at the group of kids – about six of them hanging on my every word. It was my second week at the Academy in Islington and word had got about that I was from Oz.

'Snakes innit?' said one girl.

'Snakes are pretty bad, true,' I said. 'Did you know that fifteen of the top twenty deadliest snakes in the world are from Australia?' I seemed to remember that wasn't too far from the truth, as it turned out. Not that I was overly bothered with the truth.

'But they're in the desert an' 'at, yeah?' said another girl. 'What do yer call it? The bush.'

'Oh, no,' I said. 'We'd get them in the house all the time.' I spread my arms wide. 'Metres, sorry, yards long, thick as your arm. I woke up one time and found this massive python wrapped around my leg.'

I was pleased to see that the pairs of eyes around me had widened appreciably.

'What you do?'

'Unwrapped it, of course,' I said. 'Took it out into the garden, let it go. The pythons aren't a problem. It's the eastern browns and the taipans that'll kill you soon as look at you.'

'An' you got them in the house?'

'All the time,' I lied. 'Them and red-bellied black snakes and tiger snakes and . . . and panther snakes.' I was pretty sure that panther snakes didn't exist, but what the hell. I paused and picked nonchalantly at a fingernail. 'Sea snakes are bad, but no one bothers with them because sharks are more likely to get you. Great whites, mainly.'

'And they're like everywhere in the sea, yeah?'

'You can't throw a rock without hitting one,' I replied. 'Then there's the blue-ringed octopus.'

'The what-now?'

'The blue-ringed octopus,' I said. I fiddled with my phone, brought up a YouTube video. 'Here's one. They look so cute, but they'll kill you stone dead. They're deadlier even than koalas.'

'Wha'?'

I figured I'd maybe stretched the truth just a little too far with this, but I was having fun.

'Not many people know that koalas have very sharp claws,' I said. 'They might look cute and cuddly, but if they get in the mood...' I brought my hand up to my throat and made a cutting gesture. 'Don't get a koala angry, is my best advice.'

'Wha' bout spiders?' This from someone who hadn't said anything yet.

'Big as dinner plates,' I said. 'And aggressive. Sometimes they kill pissed-off koalas, which is handy.'

There were six very satisfying (from my perspective, at least) gasps.

'Let me tell you about the drop bear,' I said.

London was a strange place until I got used to it. I thought I knew what living in a big city was like, coming from Melbourne and its five million people. London was nearly twice that. Accents were totally weird, double-decker buses everywhere, restaurants amazing and nearly as good as Melbourne's, traffic really really crazy (much quicker to walk), the Underground like something out of a movie with all those steps and tunnels and escalators that made it sometimes feel like you were journeying to the centre of the Earth. Sam had rented a two-bedroom apartment in Angel, which I thought was a super cool name for a suburb, and it was small but really expensive. Mum said it was about twice the price you'd pay to rent a similar place in Melbourne. It had central heating – these weird radiators dotted around the place with hot water running through them. No garden, but then again it was normally too cold to go outside anyway. Best to hug a radiator. There were supermarkets with strange names like Asda and Sainsbury's, though Aldi was a familiar face. You had to pay to watch the television. I don't mean there was a slot meter or anything, but you had to buy a licence, which was something crazy like three hundred bucks a year. Even if you didn't have a television but wanted to stream programs on your phone, they'd sting you with this charge. Didn't make any sense to me. Instead of using a myki card to get around, you used something called an Oyster card. It would be dark when you went to school and dark when you got home. Even when there was daylight it was dark. Cold. In summer, apparently. Especially in summer, I was informed.

And the rain. Don't get me started on the rain.

I began to love the place. It crept up on me, as love has a habit of doing.

Mum got a job as a teacher in a school that mainly dealt with 'challenged' students. She told me she challenged them to do work and they didn't. Classroom management was a nightmare. Marking was easy because they didn't do any writing.

After a few weeks of coming home and gently beating her head against the wall, she started to love the school and the students.

Sam was apparently highly thought-of in his advertising agency, which brought us all benefits. For one thing we could afford the scandalous rent in Angel, but we'd all go on trips, sometimes for work and sometimes just on outings at the weekend. Glasgow was amazing. Sam said everyone spoke English, but that wasn't my experience. I didn't understand a word the whole time I was there. We went to Stonehenge. We went to villages in places like Suffolk and Kent and Dorset and saw thatched cottages dating back hundreds of years. We explored castles. One was called Highclere Castle and Mum almost wet herself with excitement because it was the set for a television program called *Downton Abbey*, whatever that was. A guide there, spotting my Australian accent, pointed out a bit snootily that English history dated back well over a thousand years to Anglo Saxon times. I sniffed and informed him that Australian history and culture dated back over sixty thousand years. He looked suitably snoot-deflated.

One amazing Monday we went to Paris for a couple of days. I was allowed to skip school and the whole adventure was a blast. It was a few minutes' walk to the Angel Underground Station, where we caught the Northern Line to Kings Cross St. Pancras. From there we got on the Eurostar and two and a half hours later, we were in Paris. Sam had a meeting somewhere, but Mum and I wandered through the streets, walked along the Seine, saw the Eiffel Tower (at a distance) and had a wonderful meal in a restaurant where no one spoke English. Not one person. I suppose I'd assumed that most people in the world spoke enough English to look after tourists, but Sam told me that night at the hotel that the French weren't too impressed by the English or their language.

'If you *expect* them to understand or speak English, then they won't,' he said. 'Most times they'll shrug and ignore you. But if you *try* to speak French they're the friendliest people.'

'Sorry, I can't speak French,' I pointed out.

'*Pardonnez-moi. Je ne parle pas français,*' he said. 'That's not beyond you. Then follow it up with "*oui*", "*non*" and "*merci*". Trust me, Cate, they'll reward you just for making an effort.'

'What about an electronic translator?'

'Only if you can find an electronic French person. Come on. What do you have to lose?'

'My dignity?'

'I hate to break it to you . . .'

I tried my few words out the following day and he was right. I mean, my accent was disgusting, but people smiled when I talked. Some even replied in English that was a million times better than my French. I was surrounded by strange places, strange people, strange buildings and a strange language. But that just made me feel . . . alive. It made me understand that worlds and possibilities were all around.

When we got back to London, it felt like coming home.

Elise and I WhatsApped constantly and rang whenever we could. The time difference caused some problems, since evening in Melbourne was morning in London and I had to get off to school. When I got back at about four in the afternoon it was around one in the morning in Australia. By the time Elise woke up it was normally past my bedtime. Ho hum. But we managed. I still worried about her. Of course I did. When your best friend tries to overdose it doesn't leave you. And distance makes you feel so . . . distanced. But she told me she was fine. Insisted on it, actually. With a few swear words thrown in. I found out that she had made friends with a boy who was new to the school. According to Elise, it was because he'd moved from London and she could quiz him about the life I'd be leading. But I know my friend. It was more than curiosity. Hey, *I* was telling her about life in London. Romance was lurking there somewhere and I was glad. I sent her postcards from everywhere I went. She sent me a postcard of Flinders Street station. Smart-arse.

Dad and I found a way to put what I still considered his betrayal behind us, though for me, at least, it lingered there in the background. We didn't talk about it. I didn't ask why he had changed his mind and he didn't volunteer the information. I knew why I didn't want to pursue it. What would I do if it turned out he had weighed up everything about having sole responsibility for a daughter and decided it wasn't worth it? Can a relationship survive that? So I told him all about London and what I was experiencing and he was really interested. I even went so far as to tell him that I thought he had been right in giving me up, that living in Europe was better than I could have imagined. Was I trying to get a bit of emotional revenge? Maybe. I'm not sure. But if I was trying to wound him, then it didn't appear to work. Dad just told me he was glad it was all going well.

I knew I was getting integrated into the Brit way of life when Mum told me I was losing my Australian accent.

'I'm not,' I said, more than a hint of resentment in my tone.

'What do you think, Sam?' Mum said.

'Yup. Definitely turning Cockney,' he said, stirring a pan of food while I laid the table. 'Give it a few months and she'll be saying, *I met this bloke, he was radio rental, know what I mean, an 'e had more rabbit than Sainsbury's, so we're walking down the frog and 'e sees someone who he says is a tea leaf, real barney rubble.*'

I knew some cockney rhyming slang, but most of this went over my head.

'Translation, please?'

'You must be mutt and jeff, Cate,' said Sam. 'Deaf. Radio rental, mental. Rabbit and pork, talk. Sainsbury's supermarket has lots of rabbit. Frog and toad, road. Tea leaf, thief. Barney rubble, trouble.'

'Clear as day,' I said. 'I'll tell Elise about it on the dog.'

'Dog and bone, phone,' said Mum and Sam together.

In early November we went to a community bonfire for Guy Fawkes Night. Apparently this guy, Guy, tried to blow up the Houses of Parliament hundreds of years ago and on the fifth of November everyone in England burns an effigy of him on a bonfire, lets off fireworks and plays with sparklers. It didn't make much sense to me, particularly since most people seemed to think Parliament was full of morons or crooks. Moronic crooks, mainly. But it turns out the politics didn't have much significance. It was just a chance to warm your hands against a big bonfire and develop red noses from the cold wind. The three of us did both.

The days passed and my birthday and Christmas were on the horizon. The air in London was getting colder and colder, which I'd thought was a physical impossibility. I'd come home from school and stick my hands in the fridge just to warm them up. I'd moan about the weather – everyone did – but I was more than a little excited to think that maybe this year I'd experience a white Christmas. Could I make angels in the snow in Angel? I came home from school one day in early December and there were flakes drifting down from a sky that seemed made of metal. It wasn't sticking, true, but it was a taste of what was to come. I couldn't wait to share it with Mum when she got home from school. But it turned out she was already home. She was home and she told me my father was dead.

# CHAPTER EIGHTEEN

★

'I'm so sorry. Please sit down, Cate.'

I didn't want to sit down.

'It's snowing,' I said.

'I know,' said Mum. 'Please sit down.'

But I didn't. I couldn't see the point in that. So I paced up and down the tiny living room. Five paces to one wall, turn around, five paces back. Repeat. Mum sat on the couch. It was a small couch because you couldn't really fit a proper size one in there. Maybe there were shops in London that specialised in miniature furniture, just to cater to people renting in apartments that were tiny. Maybe . . . But Mum was speaking. I'd missed the first bit.

'. . . that day in court,' she said. 'When your father abandoned the case. Do you remember the day before that? The first day?'

I paced up and down, up and down. There was a window in the living room and it had this lace curtain that only came halfway up, which was weird. It meant that light coming in through it had a milky hue. The top half of the window was clear and I could see flakes swirling and dancing against the gathering dark. Chips of relentless white. Playing in the wind.

'We had to finish early that day, Cate. Your father had an appointment at the hospital. We all thought it was a routine check-up after the accident. It wasn't.'

I did remember that day. Mum and I had Indian takeaway. She'd invited Dad, but he didn't want to come. It was the night of the huge fight, when Mum said that if Dad and I won, then she wouldn't leave Australia. It would've all been my fault. I couldn't remember why it would have been my fault, but the feeling was strong.

'They'd discovered he had cancer, Cate.' For the first time, I realised Mum was crying. She wasn't making crying sounds, but tears were running down her cheeks just the same. That was weird as well. 'Pancreatic cancer. Inoperable, untreatable. A death sentence. They told him that afternoon.'

I nodded. Something was making sense but I wasn't sure what it was. There was silence then for a while, but I couldn't say for how long it lasted.

'He came to court. He told his lawyer. They stopped the case.'

'Why?' It seemed an important question. Dad and I were going to win. I remember I felt that strongly, as we were sitting there waiting for him to arrive at court. The judge without her wig, the coat of arms, the heavy bench and witness box. All that serious wood. Victory was within reach. I could taste it. Mum was pacing and I was sitting on the couch. We had swapped places and I couldn't remember when that had happened.

'Your father told me about a week later. We met up in the city and he told me. He said he couldn't bear the thought of you watching him die, day by day. Getting weaker, losing weight, being in pain.' Mum put a hand to her head, rubbed above her eyes. 'He said that thought was worse than death itself. So he wanted us gone. If you were on the other side of the world, then you'd be spared the immediate pain at least. He made me swear I wouldn't tell you.'

I knew this was an important conversation. For a while there, I was . . . I don't know. Not paying attention. Lost in thoughts and memories that twirled and danced like the snowflakes outside. Drifting into nothing and nowhere. I forced myself to focus. My father was dead and I hadn't had the chance to say goodbye. My eyes were dry. So was my mouth. Mum carried on talking.

'He knew that at some time, we'd have to have this conversation, that the responsibility for breaking the news to you would fall on me.' She gave a laugh but it was kind of strangled. 'He worried about that. Thought it probably wasn't fair on me. And we discussed whether it would be better coming from his own mouth, maybe in a phone conversation when you were over here and there was no way you could go back. But he said . . . he said something like he didn't want you to spend even one day thinking about what was to come. He wanted you to enjoy every moment. Live in the present. Before the bandaid had to be ripped off. Quick pain. Quicker because it wasn't anticipated.'

'He died alone.'

Mum didn't try to argue with me. I was grateful for that. Not then, but later, when I'd had time to process all of this.

'It's what he wanted,' she said.

But no one could want that. No one wants to die alone, in some empty room where you might not be found for hours or days. Or die with someone you don't know too well, perhaps someone paid to look after you. A stranger. We all want to die in the presence of someone who cares, who will mourn, who will understand what has just passed from this world and lament that it can never return. No one should die alone. I must have spoken these words out loud, because Mum answered them.

'For him it was better to die alone than give pain to people who watched and cared.'

This was desperately sad and I was desperately tired.

'It's okay to cry, Cate,' Mum said.

'I know,' I said. 'I know. But I've given up tears, Mum. Or maybe tears have given up on me.'

I really don't remember much of the rest of the day. Sam came home at some point. Looking back, I guess Mum must have rung and given him the news. He didn't try to give me comfort. He's a wise and a kind man, is Sam. I think he wanted to give me *space*, but that was almost impossible in a tiny flat – there wasn't enough room for two adults, one teenager and an invisible mass of grief waiting in the shadows for its turn. So he said he was going for a walk. I asked if I could go too. And that's how the three of us found ourselves freezing to death, wandering the streets of Angel and watching the snow as it drifted in the final stages of its journey. I held out my hand and caught a few flakes in my palm. I remembered reading somewhere that each snowflake is unique, it has a pattern that has never been before and can never come again. I thought that was wondrous. Countless billions of flakes, all different. It wasn't a huge leap to think of the parallel. Billions of people, all different. Each with a pattern that has never been before and can never come again.

The flakes lay for a moment until the warmth of my hand reached them. Then they shrivelled and curled until all that was left was a drop of wetness. I lifted my hand to my mouth and it was cold against my tongue.

I woke in the middle of the night because tears had found me again.

Mum held me while the pain burst through and I howled. She held me tight.

# CHAPTER NINETEEN
★

Christmas.

It had been an enduring complaint that my birthday came on the twenty-third of December and that I would therefore miss out on presents. I mean, they tell you it doesn't make any difference, but it does. They pretend you'll get exactly the same amount of attention and the same number of gifts as if you were born in June or July or March or something, but it's crap. I understand it. You buy presents for Christmas. And you buy presents for the birthday, but you're not going to buy the equivalent amount. You might intend to, but you don't. That's just the nature of things and everyone born around Christmas gets it. Mainly because they don't have a choice.

'What do you want for Christmas, Cate?' Mum asked. 'And your birthday, of course.'

I thought about it. Of course I did. But I couldn't think of much. Clothes. Better yet, a voucher so I could choose my own on the grounds mothers might have strong views on teenage fashion but they are *always* wrong. A new phone? Sam, I knew, was keen to get me some suitably awesome tech. A gaming computer? That would do. I wasn't really bothered, but I knew they wanted to get me something that was guaranteed to produce a sharp intake of breath when I opened it. So I pretended to covet a super-duper, unbelievably fast laptop. It would be useful and it would give them enormous pleasure to buy it. Win-win.

My birthday was on a Friday, and if I *had* been born in June or July or March I'd have had to go to school, but school was out for Christmas. It's about the only advantage of having a birthday around that time. So when Mum asked me what I wanted to do on my birthday, I knew that she and I could do anything we wanted. Sam would be at work, but we could shop or sightsee – there were still plenty of places I hadn't been in London. Carnaby Street, famous for its fashion, was an option. Mainly known for sixties fashion, but hey, that could be really cool. I hadn't even been to Buckingham Palace and although it was unlikely I'd see any royalty while I was there, it was something every Australian *should* do, if only to say they'd done it.

'Sorry,' said Mum. 'I should have said the Saturday.'

'What's wrong with the Friday?' I asked. 'You know, my actual birthday.'

'I have something planned. On Saturday Sam and I will both be free.'

'Something planned?'

Mum waved a hand.

'Yes,' she said. 'I have a life too, Cate. And I put myself down for an in-service on teaching disadvantaged youth. Should be really good. Really helpful.'

'On my birthday?'

'They wouldn't postpone it on the grounds it was the birthday of Caitlyn Carson. I asked. They refused. Go figure.'

'So I'll be alone on my birthday?'

Mum sighed. 'For some hours, yes. How old are you, Cate? Five?'

It didn't really matter to me, but it wasn't often that the opportunity to give a parent shit came up, so I didn't want to let it go. Then I let it go.

'All good,' I said. 'Maybe the three of us could go see a show on the Saturday?'

'I'll check out what's on,' said Mum.

It's difficult to express how much I missed Elise. Talking to her wouldn't have taken away the pain of my father's death – and, more, the guilt that I wasn't there to witness it, to be there and pat his hand and say stupid things and just, just, just be a daughter when a father needs a daughter. To tell him I loved him. To hear that he loved me, though I knew he did. But a best friend is exactly what you need in that situation. And she wasn't there. It hurt. Yeah, we talked on texts and WhatsApp, but there's a reason why social media isn't any good for anything other than ... well, the stuff social media does well.

Mainly nothing to do with feelings. I talked to her on the phone sometimes, but it wasn't the same as being there, seeing her face, watching her smile, listening to her voice and seeing something special in her eyes, something that said she understood. We were half a world apart and it felt many worlds further than that.

I'd made friends at the Academy and they were cool. But they weren't friends who had earned the right to listen to what I wanted – needed – to talk about. And Mum and Sam? They were great. But they were never going to be enough. I felt lonely. Like I was in some kind of bubble, visible but also shut off from everyone and everything else. Something had died in me and no one seemed to see it, let alone understand.

What had my father been thinking when he died? Was I there in his head as he gave his last breath? Where was he? Who had been there? Who cried for him? Who dressed him for the cremation? I didn't even know where his ashes were. So many questions and no one to answer them. I thought it would break my heart.

I lay in bed on the Thursday evening and checked for messages from Elise. Melbourne was eleven hours ahead of London – in Australia it was my birthday already. But there was nothing. I tried ringing her. Like me, she would have finished school for Christmas. But it went straight to messages. So I texted her. She couldn't have forgotten it was my birthday. Could she?

I felt a bit sorry for myself. I tried to feel guilty for that, but I couldn't find one reason to. London was great, but my father was gone, my best friend wasn't answering my calls and my mother had another engagement for my birthday. Fourteen years old. Should I be more mature? Absolutely.

Then another thought hit. I suppose it had always been there but I was trying not to let it surface. Elise had always said she was okay. She'd *insisted*. But I'd missed the signs before. And her not texting or picking up the phone was a bad sign.

In the morning I felt a bit better. If something was wrong, Elise's mum would've rung. Wouldn't she? I tried to comfort myself with that thought.

Mum and Sam had made pancakes for my birthday breakfast, which brought me some way towards forgiving them. Strawberries and cream and maple syrup and crispy bacon. They got stuck in to the food as well.

'I'll worry about the calories later,' said Mum.

'Why worry about something like that?' I asked.

'Says someone who could eat four chocolate cakes and not put on an ounce.' Mum pointed her fork at me. 'I *look* at a french fry and my hips widen.'

'Too much information,' I said.

Sam washed up afterwards and then they gave me my presents. Three packages from Mum that, by their general squidginess, were clothes. Two tops, one dress.

'Beautiful,' I said.

Mum sighed.

'I have the receipts for when you take them back to exchange.'

'Why would I do that?'

'Because you hate them.'

I folded them up carefully and put them on the breakfast table.

'You have no evidence for that,' I pointed out.

'It's written on your face, Caitlyn. Everything you think and feel is written on your face.'

Something clenched inside. How long would I live with echoes of Dad and the sudden punch when I remembered I'd never see him again?

At least I didn't have to worry about facial writing when I opened Sam's gift. A super-duper, unbelievably fast laptop. It was cool. I knew there would be kids at school who would be really envious. This thing was so advanced it opened programs before you even realised you wanted them open. I'd play around with it today, while Mum and Sam did their things. And I'd ring Elise again; she still hadn't replied to any of my messages. I didn't care if it was some ungodly hour in Melbourne. I *needed* to know she was okay.

Mum looked at her watch, then handed me an envelope. My heart stopped for three or four beats.

It had my name on the front, in Dad's handwriting.

'I have instructions,' said Mum. 'And the first is to tell you that you have choices, Cate. You don't have to open that if you don't want to, if you find it too . . . upsetting. It's up to you.'

I felt the envelope in my hand. It was thin. Not a card. Maybe a couple of sheets of paper. Maybe just one. I looked up at Mum and Sam. Worry was printed on their faces.

'What's going on, Mum?'

'I don't know, Cate. I swear I don't know. I have instructions, like I said. People that I had to ring, letters I had to pass on when I got news of his death. Now I have things to say, depending on your choices. Things to do, depending on your choices. But what it's all about?' She shrugged. 'What's the story? Only your father knew. No one else.'

*The story.* It started to make sense.

'It's a game,' I said. 'A last game.'

Mum smiled. 'I thought that, too. He had time to think and plan. Time to stage one final miracle. Maybe.'

I weighed the envelope in my hand, but it wasn't a difficult choice. I couldn't throw this envelope away like I'd thrown away his last letter so many months back. I slid my finger under the seal and opened it. Mum and Sam took a step back as if what was in there might be explosive. Maybe it was. I took out a sheet of paper and another sealed envelope. I unfolded the letter.

*Happy birthday, Cate. Fourteen years old. I am so sorry I couldn't be there to join in with the celebrations. And of course I'm so sorry that the news of my death arrived in the way it did. I know your mum will have explained everything. I can only hope you will forgive me.*

*If you are reading this, then you have made your first decision. A few more will come in quick succession. In about five minutes there will be a knock on the door and a man (or a woman – there are some things that I can't plan for with any certainty) will ask if you want to go with them. This is the next choice. If all this is too upsetting, then just say, 'No, thank you', and he or she will leave. Your mother has instructions on what to do if that's the case, though basically, that will be the end and you can spend the day as you probably planned to spend it. If you decide to go with them, you will get into a car. It's then that you should open the other envelope that accompanies this letter. Your mum and Sam will get in a car that will follow yours. I did not want you to feel that strangers were taking you somewhere possibly dangerous. So your mother and Sam will be with you, but they are instructed not to interfere because these . . . experiences are intended for you and you only.*

*Whatever your choice, Cate, know that I love you and wish you the best possible birthday.*
*Love always,*
*Dad*

I folded the letter and put it back into the envelope, turned the other envelope over in my hand. There was nothing written on it. The silence in the tiny apartment was almost overwhelming.

'All of that stuff about an in-service today, Mum,' I said finally. 'That wasn't true.'

'No,' said Mum. 'That was a lie. And Sam's taken the day off. We know that something might happen, that we might be on a mystery tour, but that's all we know.' Mum pointed to the letter. 'What does that say?'

I didn't want to tell her. Part of me knew this was unfair. She and Sam were apparently players in a game and they didn't know what their role was or what they had to do, if anything. But I didn't want to say.

'What happens between me and Dad,' I replied, 'stays between me and Dad. Just like I never told him about what went on at our house.'

Mum smiled. 'I remember,' she said.

'But in a minute or two,' I said. 'There will be a knock on the door and we will be leaving.'

Mum and Sam both glanced at the door. It was almost funny.

'Where are we going?' said Sam.

'No idea,' I said. 'Sometimes you just have to surrender to story and let it take you where it will. We'll find out.'

There was a knock on the door.

# CHAPTER TWENTY

It was a woman. She had a kind face beneath a peaked cap. She was wearing a uniform.

'Caitlyn Carson?' she said.

'Yes.'

She stepped to one side and made a sweeping gesture with one arm.

'Your carriage awaits, madam,' she said. 'If you wish to come with me.'

I glanced back into the apartment. Mum and Sam both had their coats over their arms. Sam held out my coat to me. It was bloody freezing out there. I took it.

'I would love to,' I said.

I don't know if it was part of the instructions Mum had been given, but she and Sam followed a good few paces behind, as if they were afraid of tripping over whatever world I was entering. I put on my coat as we went down the one flight of stairs that led to the street.

The chauffeur, for that was what the uniform suggested to me, opened the door and I stepped outside.

The stretch limousine was parked in the middle of the street, and I imagine most times this would have had people tooting their horns and yelling and generally ramping up the road rage. But there were police officers around, organising traffic. The road we lived in had been shut at both ends, but anyone parked on the street could get out when the police opened up an exit for them. I stood for a few moments, my mouth hanging open. All this for me? It didn't make sense.

I probably would've stood there for a few more minutes if my phone hadn't buzzed and snapped me out of my daze. An incoming message. I checked it. From Elise. Thank God.

*So sorry cc. Got caught up in a trip with mum. Happy birthday will ring later.*

There were about a dozen heart emojis. I smiled and put the phone away.

The chauffeur opened the rear door of the limo for me and I slid in. Out of the corner of my eye I saw Mum and Sam getting into an ordinary car behind mine. My door closed with a whisper and a few seconds later and about a mile away, the chauffeur got behind the wheel. I looked around the limo's interior. It was all polished walnut and white leather and about the size of our entire apartment. There was even a large television in a console in front of me. There were other things but I didn't have time to check them out fully. Probably ice machines and drinks dispensers and everything the rich and famous could possibly want. Though the windows were heavily tinted, I could see outside; yet I felt cut off, in my own private world. The rest of London was at a distance.

'I've been told you would give me instructions.' The driver's voice came through an intercom device, though I couldn't see where it was.

'Instructions?' I said.

'Yes.'

Which was when I remembered the other envelope. It was still grasped tightly in my hand. I opened it and took out the one piece of paper inside.

*You are in the back of a stretch limousine. At some point, Cate, you might wonder how I came to pay for all this, so I'll answer that now. Life insurance. Insurance that sometimes pays before actual death, under certain circumstances. It doesn't matter. In time you will receive money in a trust fund. It will take care of education fees and also give you funds for travel. Enough of that boring stuff.*

*You have a choice now, Cate. If you tell the driver, 'Drive', he or she will drive off and give you a running commentary of the places you're going to. If you say, 'Play', then I'll appear on the television screen in front of you and talk. Now I know this might seem scary or unpleasant or weird. So if you choose to let the chauffeur talk to you, that's fine and understandable. Remember also that you can*

*stop this whole thing any time you want. Just tell the driver to take you home. Simple as that.*
*Are you ready, Cate?*

I took a deep breath. Was I ready? I couldn't tell. All I knew was that I was half dreading seeing my father and half desperate to do just that. Maybe I'd burst into tears. Maybe I'd close my eyes and just listen to his voice. Maybe...

'Play,' I said.

I didn't cry. I didn't close my eyes. I smiled. Then I laughed. Dad's face, just as I remembered it, maybe a touch thinner, perhaps with a few more lines around the eyes. He sat in his old chair in his old house, but I couldn't see much because his face filled a good portion of the screen. He leaned forward.

'Hello, Cate,' he said. 'Happy birthday. Happy, happy birthday.' He smiled and spread his hands out. 'I didn't know what to get you as a gift. And then I thought of this. I hope that today brings you... well, some laughs, some drama and much happiness. After the year you've had I think that's the least you deserve.'

I was aware the limousine was moving, though I couldn't hear the engine or even the tyres on the road.

'We will be moving throughout London today,' Dad continued. 'To four... I don't really know what to call them. Experiences? I remember what you said in your statement at court. That I wrote scripts, set dramas and made sure the actors were all in place. I hope that's what will happen today, but I'm relying upon everyone working together and following instructions to the letter. It might work. It might not. I guess you'll find out, Cate. We'll speak again soon. For now, enjoy the show. I think the first part might make you laugh. You were always at your best when you were laughing.'

He held up a hand to the camera.

'Pause,' he said. And the image stilled, then the screen turned to black. I don't know how that was done. Did the chauffeur press a switch up there in the front, or did whatever device doing the recording and playback operate on voice commands? I suppose it didn't matter. I lay back into the soft leather of my seat and replayed the last few minutes in my head. Seeing Dad again. It wasn't creepy, it was... it was... it was like being given a second chance at something you thought had gone forever. It felt like a gift. The best gift I could be given on my birthday.

I didn't know London well. Okay, I'd been on many buses – the big red ones that I used to think were so cool when I saw pictures of them back in Oz, but which now I didn't even really notice – but the roads are so higgledy-piggledy that it's impossible to get a sense of direction. Sam had told me that taxi drivers in London, the ones in the black cabs, had to memorise twenty-five thousand streets, three hundred and twenty routes and twenty thousand landmarks and places of interest before getting their licence to drive.

'That's nuts,' I'd said. 'Why not use sat nav?'

'Not allowed to. It's all done by memory. They call it The Knowledge.'

I didn't have The Knowledge. I had The Ignorance. After ten minutes I had no idea where we were. But after eighteen, a penny dropped. We were in The Mall, the road leading up to Buckingham Palace, and there in front of us was the statue of Queen Victoria with its wonderful gold topping of angels or something and behind it the palace itself. The home of Britain's royal family. I had images of us driving up to the gates, which would open because a stretch limousine *demands* entry, passing through that archway and being greeted by a posse of minor and major royalty, possibly with a birthday cake in hand.

That didn't happen. We stopped by the statue of Queen Victoria and the driver told me to let myself out and stand by the car door.

I did. It was strange because there were loads of tourists around and they all turned towards me. I guess there was bugger-all activity inside the palace and I had to be someone important with a car like that. A good number took photographs of me as I stood there looking and feeling like an idiot. Maybe they thought I was a rock star. So I waved at them. I still felt like an idiot but at least I now had a reason to feel that way. Some people waved back. More pics were taken. It was getting silly.

Around the corner, a horse-drawn carriage appeared. It was kinda fancy – bits of gold work on the edges. It stopped a few metres away and the Queen got out. She adjusted her crown, which had slipped a little as she was getting down from the carriage. A corgi followed. The tourists gaped. Some even forgot to take photographs.

The Queen stepped up to me.

'You must be Caitlyn Carson,' she said in that trademark plummy accent.

I laughed.

'That's me,' I replied. The Queen frowned.

'Ma'am,' she said rather haughtily. 'You should say, "That's I, Ma'am".'

I thought I would wet myself with laughter, but managed to control myself.

'Sorry, Ma'am,' I said.

The Queen smiled, revealing startlingly white dentures.

'That's better,' she said. 'Well, happy birthday, Caitlyn Carson. If we all just hop orf into your car, I'll take you for a bite of lunch at a rather fine establishment I know in Hampstead. What do you say?'

I opened the limo door.

'I'd be honoured, Ma'am,' I said.

# CHAPTER TWENTY-ONE

★

I'd read about celebrity doubles. I think I'd even read about the Queen double and how she made a decent living just by wandering around in pearls, dragging a dog and waving gently with one hand, its palm turned towards her face. Up close, she was great. Not exactly like the proper Queen, of course, but near enough to be fun.

She settled into the seat next to me, the dog curled at her feet, and our limo took off into traffic again.

'I do hope Trixie here has got over her intestinal issues,' said the Queen. 'She's been farting worse than Charles lately.'

You know the kind of laughter where nasty stuff wants to explode from your nostrils? I got that. For nearly a minute. The Queen patted my leg.

'You are from the Antipodes, I believe,' she said.

'Yes,' I gurgled. 'Melbourne.'

'Been there,' she said. 'Been everywhere really. Melbourne? Yes, seem to remember it. Everyone crazy about coffee but no one wants to actually drink it because instead they ask for triple-skim venti non-fat caramel macchiato. And you think us Brits are up our own arses! Pardon my French, dear.'

I giggled uncontrollably.

The car ride took about half an hour and the Queen and I chatted. Nearly everything she said made me laugh. Then I wondered what Mum and Sam must have thought when they saw the Queen getting into the back of the limo with me and I laughed some more.

'You do a lot of laughing, dear,' said the Queen. 'It's starting to give me a headache.'

We finally stopped in a narrow street in a part of London I didn't recognise. Hampstead was supposed to be posh. This area wasn't. It was the kind of place full of breakfast bars selling bacon and egg sandwiches and dodgy burgers. The Queen, her corgi and I alighted outside one called Harry's Nosh Bar.

We entered. A large and sweaty man behind a large and probably sweaty counter slung a soiled and certainly sweaty tea towel over his shoulder and greeted us. Rather, he greeted the Queen.

''Ello darlin',' he said. 'Long time no see. 'Ow's it hanging then?'

'Hello Harry,' said the Queen. 'And I think you mean, "How's it hanging, Ma'am?"'

'You're right and no mistake,' said Harry. 'So,

Ma'am. Table for two and a saveloy for the Hound of the Baskervilles, yeah?'

We had sausages, bacon, chips, fried eggs, baked beans, black puddings and thick slices of toast. This was a heart attack on a plate and I loved it. The Queen kept up a constant patter, telling me all sorts of scandalous things about the royal family and telling me what she really thought about some of its members.

'Don't get me started on the ginger toerag, dear,' she said, and I spat a piece of sausage across the table and onto the floor. Luckily, the corgi was on full alert for circumstances like this. When we finished the Queen paid with a twenty-pound note. 'My bloody picture's everywhere,' she said as she held the note up to the light. 'And I don't even get royalties.'

The limo was waiting for me. I offered the Queen a lift.

'That's okay, dear,' she said. 'I'll get an Uber. Or better still, I'll get that lazy skid mark, William, to come and pick me up. Orf you go.' And she closed the door on me.

I was still laughing when we turned the corner and she was lost to sight.

What had Dad said? Four experiences. Well, that was one down and three to go. I hoped the others didn't involve eating. I didn't think I'd eat for the rest of my life.

Dad's face appeared on the monitor.

'How's the birthday going, Cate? I really hope what I planned so far has come off, but of course I'll never know. Even if it hasn't, then I suppose you'll know what I *tried* to accomplish. That's something.' He scratched his nose. 'Anyway. On to Hyde Park. You've probably been to the most famous park in London a few times. I'm hoping things will be a bit different for you this time. Of course, I also hope that the weather is kind. If it's belting down with rain, then there will be waterproofs and an umbrella in the car. Maybe for once the London weather will be okay, though the odds are always against it. And it's four days before Christmas, so it's bound to be freezing. I hope you're well bundled up against the cold. Enjoy and see you after Hyde Park.' And he held up his hand again. 'Pause.'

I knew Hyde Park was close to Buckingham Palace and wondered whether I'd bump into Her Majesty returning. I didn't. The limo drove right into the grounds and stopped in some place called the Princess Diana Memorial Fountain car park. The chauffeur got out and opened the door. She pointed out a path to the left of a circular waterway and said that at the end I would find a statue called *Serenity*, a tribute to the late Princess Diana. I was to wait there and when everything was over to come back here. I nodded and walked off. Out of the corner of my eye I saw Mum and Sam's car pull up. They got out and followed me, a decent distance behind. It was good to see them, but it was also good to still be basically alone. I put my hands into my coat pockets because I'd forgotten my gloves. It was so cold and snowflakes were starting to fall. I got the strong feeling that these ones were going to stick. When I looked at the sky it seemed packed with darkness and the guarantee of more snow. But that hadn't put people off visiting the park. Joggers, walkers, people sitting on benches probably literally freezing their butts off. It was a busy place.

It wasn't difficult to find *Serenity*. It was a huge bronze bird, its beak arched over its back. It was so beautiful and peaceful that it wasn't hard to understand how it got its name. Beyond the statue was a river. Though my knowledge of London wasn't the best, I figured this was the Serpentine. At the base of the statue, sitting cross-legged, was a young man playing a flute. I recognised the tune and I smiled. This is why I was here.

Back in Australia, Dad and I had sometimes watched flash mobs on YouTube. Mainly, these amazing videos where a full orchestra appeared from buildings lining an ordinary street, one instrument at a time, in front of amazed and unsuspecting onlookers who were then treated to a beautiful and moving version of a classic. Dad loved those videos. I felt a shiver run up my spine because I guessed what was coming.

The young man was playing a tune based on a children's song called 'Kookaburra', but it was best known as a riff in the song 'Down Under' by the Australian band Men At Work. He played gently, the riff repeating. It was a beautiful and haunting tune. Then, out of thin air, it seemed, the flute was joined by a bass guitar. A man appeared out of bushes to my left and he stepped up to the side of the flautist. By this time, a crowd was gathering and phones were being raised. I wished they wouldn't. I just wanted to enjoy this and, in some strange fashion, maybe the tourists and locals understood because they didn't block my view, though they screened things enough that I didn't see the lead guitarist or the keyboard player or the drummer as they appeared one by one. Where the hell had someone hidden a set of drums? I laughed.

And then they started to sing 'Down Under'. It was brilliant and I found myself once again on the verge of tears. More and more people had gathered now – maybe seventy or eighty – and they formed a semicircle around the five performers. I supposed I should have seen it coming – the fact that the gap in the circle gave me a clear line of sight was a massive clue. But I didn't. Not until the song was over and I started to applaud. Then the whole crowd turned towards me as the band struck up the opening chords of another song.

I stood as seventy or eighty people sang, 'Happy birthday to you. Happy birthday, Cate Carson. Happy birthday to you.' I couldn't help it. The whole scene before me became misted. I blinked and my vision steadied. When the song was done, the crowd mingled together, wandered off, didn't look at me. Within twenty seconds they were just a bunch of tourists and locals wandering around a park, going about their business and leaving me to mine.

'Do you remember when we went to that amazing place outside Melbourne, Cate? Where we watched the crowded night sky and UFOs turned up to say hello?'

I smiled. That was an evening I would never forget and I'm pretty sure Dad understood that.

'I pointed out Betelgeuse to you and said that we were witnessing time travel.' Dad smiled on the screen. 'That's where we're going now, Cate. Not to another star. God, I would've *loved* to have organised that. No. Something a bit more . . . ordinary. Back to a time when the light from Betelgeuse had started its journey, but wasn't very far into it. Think of this limousine as a time machine.' He smiled. 'Hey, that rhymes. I'm a poet and I didn't know it. Enjoy the past, Cate, and become a playing part of it.' He held up his hand again. 'Pause.'

The snow was getting thicker outside, and even though it wasn't quite two in the afternoon, the day was becoming darker and darker. I squinted through the car's tinted windows and saw Big Ben approaching. We kept turning every few hundred metres – the chauffeur either had The Knowledge or a decent sat nav system – so the building would appear and then disappear. I knew the Houses of Parliament were close to the famous clock tower, the very same parliament that old Guy Fawkes had tried to blow up hundreds of years before. And then we were travelling over a bridge, the River Thames below us, the Houses of Parliament and Big Ben now behind.

South of the Thames. Back in time? I hadn't a clue.

Until the building appeared – an amazing black and white building with wooden beams and rafters dotted on the outside – and we slowed and stopped in front of it.

The Globe Theatre. Not the original Globe that Shakespeare used to act in – that had burned down, been rebuilt and then destroyed almost four hundred years ago. This replica of the original was constructed maybe twenty-five years ago – and only a few hundred metres from Shakespeare's original stage. Time travel.

The chauffeur opened the door for me and I stepped out into bitter cold. She took me up a flight of steps to where a young woman was waiting.

'You must be Caitlyn Carson,' said the woman. 'Please follow me. Wardrobe and make-up are ready for you.'

Dad's words came back to me. *Become a playing part of it*. He wasn't expecting me to act in front of an audience. Was he?

I stepped into the theatre and stopped. It was miraculous. The theatre was open to the sky and there was a raised stage made of old interlocked planks. At the back of the playing area were doors, panels and pillars of the most amazing colours. Above them was a second floor with balconies overlooking the stage. But as I raised my head it was the roof above the stage that took my breath away. Glorious panels of the heavens painted in a deep shade of blue with stars, planets and the signs of the zodiac.

I turned one-eighty degrees. Behind me were three tiers of seating.

'That's where the people with money would watch the plays,' said the woman at my side. 'Where we're standing now is the Pit. Where the commoners would pay a penny to watch Shakespeare's plays. They called the commoners 'groundlings', partly because they were on the ground but also because a groundling was a type of fish known for lurking at the bottom of rivers.' She took my arm. 'Anyway. Come on. Time is moving.'

At least the theatre was empty – apart from the figures of Mum and Sam, who entered just as I was being led backstage.

No one really talked too much in the costume department. One man looked at me, put a finger to his mouth and then plucked an outfit from the rack behind. It was the most glorious, full-length gown, made of some kind of heavy red material. There were lacy things at the cuffs and white embroidery down the front panel. It weighed a ton. After I got changed, someone placed a chunky gold crucifix on a chain around my neck and then I was led to make-up. That didn't take long either. An unsmiling, fiercely concentrating woman applied some white pan to my face and then painted a red circle on each cheek. There wasn't much exposed flesh to deal with. The costume covered everything.

A man came in as we were finishing and introduced himself as John, one of the directors at the Globe. At least he was smiling and friendly.

'I suppose you're wondering what this is about,' he said.

'I'm about to be in a play, but I have no idea what it is or who I'm meant to be,' I replied.

He smiled.

'Luckily, you don't need any of that information. Just answer me one thing. Can you read?'

I cocked my head and gave him a death stare, but that didn't appear to dampen his good mood.

'I'll take that as a yes,' John said. 'Excellent. I think you're getting into character already. Follow me.'

And he took me up a flight of stairs. Even though I was slightly disorientated, I had the impression I was above the stage and that the door in front of me would lead to one of the balconies just below the gloriously painted roof. I tried to stay calm and keep my breathing regular.

'It's very simple,' said John. 'When you go through that door, you step up to the edge of the balcony. Just below the railing, on your side of it, you'll see a clear perspex panel. Very much like an autocue. Your lines will appear there. Just speak them as best you can. Don't worry about volume.' He smiled. 'This might look like a theatre from four hundred years ago, but it has the best technology beneath its old-fashioned exterior. Any questions?'

*Only about a thousand*, I thought.

'There isn't an audience out there, is there?' I said.

John smiled.

'Naturally. An audience of two in the Pit. Your parents, I believe?' I didn't correct him. 'This is just fun, Cate. Enjoy yourself and don't worry. Good to go?'

Probably not, but I opened the door anyway.

For once, my sense of direction had worked. I was below the heavens but above the stage. Directly in front of me was a row of seating on the second floor. I stepped up to the railing and looked down. Mum and Sam stood in the very centre of the Pit. Even at a distance I could see their eyes widen as they looked up at me. I glanced down at the screen. Two words appeared. I took a breath.

'Ay, me,' I said. My voice rang out across the theatre.

A young man appeared from the bottom row of seating, directly across from me. He darted across the Pit and stood almost by the side of Mum. He had on tights, knee-length boots and a white shirt unbuttoned to his navel.

'She speaks,' he said in hushed tones. 'O, speak again, bright angel, for thou art as glorious to this night, being o'er my head, as is a winged messenger of heaven unto the white-upturned wondering eyes of mortals that fall back to gaze on him when he bestrides the lazy-puffing clouds and sails upon the bosom of the air.'

I knew this play. I had studied it. Now I was in it. I looked down at my screen but knew that there were some parts already locked in my head.

'O Romeo, Romeo! Wherefore art thou Romeo?' I said. 'Deny thy father and refuse thy name; or, if thou wilt not, be but sworn my love, and I'll no longer be a Capulet.'

The actor took a step towards me.

'Shall I hear more, or shall I speak at this?'

I put my hands against my heart.

"Tis but thy name that is my enemy.' I looked over the heads of those below as if talking to the sky itself. 'Thou art thyself, though not a Montague. What's Montague? It is nor hand, nor foot, nor arm, nor face, nor any other part belonging to a man. O, be some other name. What's in a name? That which we call a rose by any other name would smell as sweet; so Romeo would, were he not Romeo called, retain that dear perfection which he owes without that title. Romeo, doff thy name, and for that name, which is no part of thee, take all myself.'

Romeo stepped forward and called up to me.

'I take thee at thy word,' he said. 'Call me but love, and I'll be new baptised; henceforth I never will be Romeo.'

I started and recoiled as if words from the darkness had shocked me.

'What man art thou that, thus bescreened in night, so stumblest on my counsel?'

'By a name,' he replied, 'I know not how to tell thee who I am: my name, dear saint, is hateful to myself, because it is an enemy to thee. Had I it written, I would tear the word.'

I stepped forward and looked down into his face.

'My ears have yet not drunk a hundred words of thy tongue's uttering, yet I know the sound. Art thou not Romeo, and a Montague?'

He held his arms up towards me.

'Neither, fair saint, if either thee dislike.'

The director stepped out onto the stage.

'Cut,' he said. 'Bravo, everyone.' He turned and looked up at me, applauded. Mum and Sam did likewise. Romeo gave me a low bow and blew me a kiss. I curtsied.

On my way out, after I'd changed and got rid of the make-up, the woman who'd ushered me in gave me a flash drive.

'Your performance,' she said. 'Happy birthday.'

When the limousine had been driving for less than a minute, Dad's face appeared for what I feared was going to be the last time.

'Oh, Cate,' he said. 'I really hope it's been a fun day for you. And I have just one more thing.' He laughed. 'Well, two, but one's merely a snippet of information. The other is an experience, though not like the others you've had today. It's really a simple gift, but I have a feeling it's one you're going to like very much. The driver is taking you to a park very close to your home in Angel. You've almost certainly been there. It's called Islington Green and it's small.' I *had* been there. I knew it. 'There is a war memorial in that park that's constructed like a circle twisting in on itself. You will go there and your gift will be behind it. The limousine will leave you when you get to the park, but it will be a short walk home. If the weather's really bad, I dare say your Mum and Sam will get an Uber or something. Enjoy. I will speak to you one more time when we get to the park. Pause.'

The dark screen once more. At least I'd see him one more time. It occurred to me to ask the chauffeur if there was a recording of this that I could take home with me, but I knew Dad wouldn't have arranged that. Speaking to me from the grave once was more than enough, he would've thought. Anything else . . . not a chance.

I opened the window – it slid down without any noise – and I held out my hand. The snow was falling heavier now and I could see the streets becoming dusted with white. It was a strange vision, the sky getting darker, the streets getting lighter by the second.

The limousine glided to a stop in a street opposite the park. It hadn't taken long to get there from the theatre – around fifteen minutes, I guessed. There wasn't much green – a few trees, a patch of lawn, some benches and the monument. The screen came to life.

'Time for me to say goodbye, Cate,' said Dad. 'At least we got the chance to do that, hey? Go find your present. Enjoy your day. Enjoy your life. And don't forget to play, Cate. Every day. If you do, you'll never grow old.' He smiled. 'Didn't George Bernard Shaw say that? Oh, and speaking of old GBS, keep on writing. Do not waste your gift. That would be tragic.' He held up his hand as if to cut the recording, then stopped. 'Oh, yes. The snippet of information I promised. The UFOs we saw that day outside Melbourne. I didn't arrange that, Cate. I swear. You probably thought you'd solved their mystery, but you hadn't. Isn't that cool?' And this time when he held up his hand, the screen went dark.

The chauffeur was very nice. She didn't make me get out of the car until I'd stopped crying. They weren't horrible tears. They were part pain, part joy. Dad was right. At least we'd said goodbye. There was something . . .

miraculous in that. And writing. Yes. If Dad taught me anything, it was that stories are all around us, that they are precious and must be honoured. There *were* stories in me. And I'd write them. For him and for me. It would be a present to both of us.

I got out of the car. The chauffeur smiled, wished me a happy birthday, got into the front and drove away. Off to my left I saw Mum and Sam standing at the side of the road, looking at me. I had no idea what kind of a day they'd had, following me around London, being a part of Dad's gift but also apart from it. We'd talk about it. When the time was right, we'd talk about it.

I stepped into the park and walked towards the memorial. It was a strange construction, but curiously pleasant, kind of doughnut shaped with the outer rim curving over itself. There was a dark shape in the centre of the doughnut's hole. As I got to within a metre or two, the shape stepped forward.

Elise.

My friend Elise, smiling and crying and holding out her arms to me. The next moment I was in them. We hugged for what seemed like hours, then we hugged some more. Finally I took a step back and wiped at my eyes.

'My father,' I said.

'Yeah,' said Elise. 'First-class plane tickets for me and Mum. Five-star hotel not far from here. Not going back until the middle of January. How good's that?'

'Wondered why you hadn't wished me a happy birthday.'

'Sorry. Thirty-five thousand feet and all that stuff.'

'Who's looking after the dog?'

Elise smiled.

'Dad. He's moved back in. Just till we get home, nothing permanent, thank God. But I reckon he's fallen in love with her. Not surprising really. They have a lot in common, him and CC.'

'CC?'

'Told you. I had to have a CC in my life.' She looked around and shivered. 'I never knew anywhere could be this freaking cold,' she said. 'But the snow is beyond cool.' She grabbed my arm. 'See what I did there? Beyond cool.'

'You're a stand-up comedian.'

Elsie took a step back.

'What's happened to your accent?'

'Nothing.'

'Like hell, nothing. You're talking weird, CC. Stop it.'

I put on my best cockney accent.

'You're 'aving a laugh at my expense,' I said. 'Do leave it out, know wha' I mean?'

We started walking towards Mum and Sam, who were still holding off. Even in the dark, though, I could see they were beaming. There was a woman next to them. Elise's mum. She was beaming, too.

'We are going to go out for a big birthday meal tonight,' I said. 'And then I'm going to tell you all about the amazing day I've had. You won't believe it.'

'You'll show me on your phone,' said El.

'Ah,' I said. 'Bit of a problem there.'

Elise smacked herself on the side of the head.

'You didn't take pictures? Videos? You know, like any freaking normal person would've done?' The last five words built in volume, so that the final syllable was a blast in my ear.

'I know. I'm an idiot.'

'True that, CC.'

'But I didn't think. At the time I was too busy experiencing it all, you know?'

'You didn't think? True that, CC.'

'I love you, El.'

'Course you do,' said Elise. 'You might be stupid, but you're not crazy.'

My hand closed on the flash drive of my performance at the Globe. At least someone had preserved some part of my day. I thought Elise would enjoy it.

I stopped just as we were getting close to the road where everyone was waiting.

'Lie down, El,' I said.

'What's that now?'

So I lay down where I knew the grass had been, but which was now a layer of snow a couple of centimetres deep. Elise smiled and lay down next to me. We held hands.

And we made snow angels in a park in Angel.

# ACKNOWLEDGEMENTS

As always, I would like to thank my team at Allen & Unwin, especially my editor, Kate Whitfield, for her customary care and sensitive attention to detail. A number of people read drafts of this book – my wife, Anita Jonsberg, is always my first reader and she made many suggestions to make Cate's story better. Even more important is her constant support during times when writing isn't going so well. Good friend (and brilliant writer) Scot Gardner took time out of his busy schedule to read my first draft and I am grateful both for his enthusiasm for this story, as well as his insights into how it could be improved. The inimitable Lesley Reece AM, founder and ex-director of The Literature Centre in Fremantle, WA, also read this book in its early stages and I am grateful for her belief in me and her unwavering devotion to all things to do with children's literature.

My friend and local Darwin lawyer, Jude Lee, gave up valuable time to advise me on matters relating to family law. All that is accurate in this book is because of him. All that isn't (and he suggested some areas where my depiction of the law stretched the truth somewhat) is my responsibility alone. I hope he enjoys being a character in this book . . .

## ABOUT THE AUTHOR

Barry Jonsberg has won numerous awards for his books, both nationally and internationally. He has been published in eighteen countries and translated into many languages. His bestselling novel, *My Life As An Alphabet*, was recently made into an award-winning film, *H is For Happiness*, released throughout the world to great critical acclaim. The same production company is now working on television and film adaptations of his last two novels, *A Song Only I Can Hear* and *Catch Me If I Fall*.

Barry lives in Darwin, in the Top End of Australia, with his wife Anita and his crazy dog, Zorro.

'A page-turner with important themes that will hook younger readers.'
*Sydney Morning Herald*

'Many unexpected twists and turns with a cliff-hanger like no other. This is a great read for readers 10+ . . . strap in and enjoy the ride.'
*Better Reading*

'[Jonsberg's] latest book charms and thrills . . . clever and unexpected. Highly recommended.'
*Reading Time*

'The kind of coming-of-age story readers will latch onto with a love and enthusiasm that is boundless . . . Jonsberg has raised the already very high bar. Give this book to everybody – it is urgent fiction and a true must-read.'
*Books + Publishing*

'Rob is a unique character in teenage fiction and one who endears himself to the reader immediately. Highly recommended.'
*Magpies*

'I will be forever grateful for Barry Jonsberg's writing, which opens doors I didn't even know were closed.'
*Kids' Book Review*

'In My Life as an Alphabet, Barry Jonsberg has an uncanny ability to take on the persona of a very special 12-year-old girl and to keep the reader totally entertained from chapters A to Z.'
*The Courier Mail*

WINNER: Victorian Premier's Literary Award
WINNER: Gold Inky Award
HONOUR BOOK: CBCA Book of the Year, Younger Readers
SHORTLISTED: Prime Minister's Literary Awards, Prize for Children's Fiction